WHAT'S HAPPENING IN FRIENDSVILLE?

A Collection of Downhome Short Stories

We love you Ruby, you are a very nice person to know

By Pearle Blaylock

Pearle Blaylock
2/7/98

Paint Rock Publishing, Inc.
Kingston, Tennessee
1997

WHAT'S HAPPENING IN FRIENDSVILLE?

A Collection of Downhome Short Stories

Paint Rock Publishing, Inc.
Kingston, Tennessee
1997

John M. Wilson
Paint Rock Publishing
118 Dupont Smith Lane
Kingston, Tennessee 37763
(423) 376-3892

Library of Congress
Cataloging-in-Publication Data

Blaylock, Pearle, 1917-
What's Happening in Friendsville: A Collection of Down- Home Stories / by Pearle Blaylock
p. cm
ISBN 0-9649394-4-4

1. United States—Short Stories—various subjects—Illustrated with photographs from Museum of Appalachia—Fiction. I. Title.
Library of Congress Cataloging in Publication
Number 97-69280

Manufactured in the United States of America
First Edition

PHOTOGRAPH CREDITS

All photographs courtesy John Rice Irwin, Museum of Appalachia, Norris, Tennessee

Cover. Spring plowing in the garden at the Museum of Appalachia, April, 1995. Photo by John Rice Irwin.

Page vi. Log house built about 4 miles N.E. of Clinchport, Virginia, near the Clinch River. It was built in the early 1800s by the Carter family. Logs were all poplar—very heavy wall plates. Photo by John Rice Irwin.

Page 4. Sally Scruggs churning butter. Photo by Frank Hoffman.

Page 8. Hill reunion, Knox County, Thomas Weaver Road, 1931. This photo shows Marcellus Rice holding a one-year old John Rice Irwin, 3rd row, 4th from right. Photographer unknown.

Page 15. Sam Jones store. Photo by Frank Hoffman.

Page 19. Ruby Allen, a craftsperson at the Tennessee Fall Homecoming. Photo by Frank Hoffman.

Page 28. Musicians on the porch at the Museum of Appalachia. From the left, seated, Alverta Stooksbury, Kyle Irwin, Carl Bean, Ron English, Charlie Acuff, and Grace Rutherford. Standing are Kay Rutherford, Carlock Stooksbury, and Sherry English. Photo by Frank Hoffman.

Page 32. Truck being used as a woodshed on the road between Pineville and Williamsburg, Kentucky. Photo in 1992 by John Rice Irwin.

Page 36. Leatherwood Church in Leatherwood Hollow, Claiborne County, 1978, photo by Mr. and Mrs. William R, Miller and property of John Rice Irwin.

Page 49. Photo taken in 1955 at Napoleon (Nap) Graves' place in Union County, Big Valley. Man is Nap's son-in-law. Photo by John Rice Irwin.

Page 67. Picture from glass negative; old Mordicai Lincoln home at auction, 1970 in Greenville, Tennessee, once the home of President Andrew Johnson's daughters. Photographer unknown; property of John Rice Irwin.

Page 80. Snow scene at Mark's Cabin at the Museum of Appalachia during the "100-year snow", March 20, 1993. Photo by John Rice Irwin.

Page 120. Log smokehouse from old McSpadden place, west of Lenoir City near the Smoky Mountains in Spring, 1991. Photo by John Rice Irwin.

Page 125. Outhouse for Springdale Baptist Church, 4 miles east of Tazewell, October, 1979. Photo by John Rice Irwin.

Page 130. Bob Douglas playing the fiddle at the Museum of Appalachia, 1988. Photo by Frank Hoffman.

Page 132. Tyler Bunch, 1978. Photo by John Rice Irwin.

Page 138. Picture from glass negative of house and family, bought at the old Mordicai Lincoln home at public auction about 1970 in Greeneville, Tennessee, once home of President Andrew Johnson's daughters. Photographer unknown; property of John Rice Irwin.

Page 184. Home of Christopher Columbus Wright on Powell River near Oak Grove in Claiborne County. Photo by Mr. and Mrs. William R. Miller and property of John Rice Irwin.

INTRODUCTION

WHAT'S HAPPENING IN FRIENDSVILLE?

REFLECTIONS

Acknowledgements

I would like to thank my husband Everet for all his love and support during the years it has taken to write these stories and in all my undertakings. John Wilson, my publisher, was instrumental in getting this book into print. Mr. Ric Wilson of Main Street Design did a great job in book layout and cover design, and Ms. Elizabeth Nash did the final editing with a delicate pen.

My daughters Nancy Blaylock and Marian Pickney and my son Everet Wyatt have supported me in all these efforts as have Marian's husband Charles and Everet's wife Betty. My three grandchildren Lou and Matthew and Mary Beth have provided love and support, I would like to dedicate this book to all these, my family.

Pearle Blaylock
September, 1997

WOW! WHAT AM I SEEING?

I got up early as usual, got my housecoat out of the closet, and put my feet in my houseshoes. I combed my hair and picked up my glasses off the dresser where I lay them each night. Then I was off to the bathroom. After washing my face of the cream that I put on each night to try to guard off the "old age look," I looked more closely into the mirror on the medicine cabinet that hangs over the lavatory. I saw something I hadn't noticed before. What was that on my upper lip? I soon figured it out, much to my amazement. Well, you guessed it: it was wrinkles, more wrinkles, and most wrinkles. They were all there. They looked like the spirals on the head of the Statue of Liberty's crown.

I stepped on the scales, which never lie, to see if the half of the cherry pie, two baked potatoes with plenty of toppings, six chocolate drop cookies, plus the other food that I eat daily for nutrition had put any extra weight on my aging body. Actually I was so confused over the upper lip wrinkles I forgot what I weighed. I made my way to the kitchen where I always have a cup of Swiss Mocha first thing. It seems to get my energy back in motion. While I sat drinking my mocha and half listening to the TV that sits on a shelf over the kitchen table, my other half was brooding over my thickly wrinkled lip.

I got to thinking just what caused all those deep wrinkles. But before getting into figuring that out, the disadvantages of the wrinkles are horrible! Here is one in particular: after you put lipstick on, some way or another the lipstick runs uphill making little red lines that jump out all over the upper lip. It makes you think of the little uniforms that candy cane girls wear when they work at the hospital.

After finishing my mocha I settled down and started my little job putting it all together where all those wrinkles came from. The first wrinkle under my nose is one from when I was a little girl. One of our mules ran after me as I raced for the barn gate. I tripped over a rock, fell flat on the ground, and cut a gash in my knee. Well, I guess I needed stitches, but I didn't want Mama sewing it up and there wasn't a hospital within 20 miles. Some kind of home remedy was applied and my knee was tied up with a piece of an old clean sheet. It didn't get infected and I didn't get "lock jaw" but I still have the scar and that wrinkle on my lip to remind me of the mule and my sore leg. I got out of carrying wood and running to the spring for water for a few days.

I'm pretty sure that three or four wrinkles were caused by my worrying that my older sisters would tell my daddy on me for things I did in school. Sometimes older sisters are a nuisance to younger ones. Especially when they are so refined and I wasn't even fine. Being good is good, but sometimes being good is so hard to do it can cause wrinkles, too.

Later when we had all grown up and moved away from the childhood home where we were all born and raised, several of the little pesky wrinkles were formed as we left. Leaving all my friends and relatives behind was very hard.

Oh, yeah–I know what formed some more of them. George, my husband-to-be, decided to go back in service. He was discharged from the Navy with a medical disability. In fact, he was injured in World War II. He got in the Merchant Marines but disagreed with the ship's cook and then got out. He came back to Tennessee and we were thrown together again. In a while, we were married. After six years we had our first child, a daughter, then another daughter and later a son.

To all you mothers, children are a blessing but they will really put wrinkles on your upper lip. You worry if they sneeze, burp up their milk, or cry out in the night. They grow up and go to school. Here come more wrinkles. Will they make good grades? Will they get along with teachers and friends? They grow up, through grammar school and high school and off to college. That causes wrinkles. You wonder if their clothes look as good as others. That makes another wrinkle.

Soon they're off on their own, and they're too busy to call, while daddy or mother are home and retired and wonder how they are doing. Parents are getting old and to the children we're getting childish. They complain about being checked on, not realizing it's just pure love and not just being nosy. To all you out there, if your parents are living, don't get annoyed when they check on you. They're not trying to run your life. They're just trying to keep an extra wrinkle from forming on their upper lip.

So long!

See ya!

HEY! WHO IS THAT TALKING?

I won't say I heard a voice, or that my inner being took over, but something happened. I had just finished sewing crocheted lace on an old tubed meal sack. I had taken great pains in cutting the sack right through the center. I carefully hemmed it, then I sewed on the lace. I had plenty of time to re-live the life of the old sack.

The old sack told me just how it thought, and here's the story, just as it was and is: The sack said, "I lived in the same house, on the same country farm, for many years. Each time the family ran short of meal, the girls and sometimes the father picked me off the railing that ran around the staircase upstairs–that's where I usually stayed–and carried me to the crib, and corn was shelled and filled almost to the top of me. They left just enough room to be tied with a twine string. There was always more excitement when the girls did the shelling. Most of the time there were heated arguments over who wasn't working as hard as the others. At times it almost came to slaps and knocks, and whoever was getting the worse end of the heated argument tried getting revenge by calling mama. Always the same words: 'Mama, make her quit.' At times even spitting became popular.

"Then I was thrown across a sweaty work horse and taken to a flour mill, where the corn was ground into meal. The miller took his toll and, after Newton exchanged a little gossip, he would throw me back on the horse with less weight than he had come down with. This happened through the 1920's and 30's.

"No one ever told me I was a pretty sack. I had bright blue and red stripes down the length of me, and as time passed, and I was washed and boiled in strong lye soap, my stripes faded.

"Why did you have me packed away in a box in a hot attic? Was it because everything was getting modern and meal could be bought already ground with the other ingredients added? I'll tell you, I resent all these modern things. They put me completely out of sight, smothered in a hot box in summer and freezing in winter. I'm afraid my threads are getting weak and worn after being put away for so long just because your husband preferred going out for public jobs instead of being a farmer so I could be useful. But you both had experienced farm work, and better days were lying ahead.

"I've got more to tell you, and you'd better listen. What I was used for made you, a corn-fed girl, and, old lady, it hasn't worn off. You're country, and regardless of how much make-up you use, you are still country. It stands out like a sore thumb. The cornbread and hot sun shining on you and your hoe handle rubbing on your hands has caused you to be as rough as the threads in my sack.

"I've seen you climb fences and apple trees, ride work horses, run like a race horse, and eat like one of the pigs in the pen. You never seemed to be tired, and you never gained a pound; you were slim and trim and full of your mischief, inherited from your father and grandfather. Oh, yeah, you loved to play pranks on people.

"Time has taken its toll on you, old lady. I've observed, and I have seen that your steps have slowed down. When you go to the mailbox, you never run like you used to and by the time you pull up the hill, your breathing sounds like distant thunder. Hard, isn't it? I've noticed at times you rub your arms: does your arthritis bother you? Why are your legs getting blue streaks in them, like the blue threads in my sack? Well, it's called varicose veins. Own up to it, old sister, years have a gib clutch on you, and what is that white stuff around your face? It's not the powder you still smear on to look young. I'll bet you don't know, but I'm going to tell you. It's your hair, it's getting gray. Admit it woman, you're not a spring chicken anymore. I've seen you teeter and totter around, and then look to see if anyone saw you. I also know you resent being considered old, but accept it–your youth went out the door many years ago. You are a great fighter. Keep it up; even if you;re rich, money can't bring back your youth when you're old. The only thing you're rich in is your memories. Yeah, memories of yesterday. In the present, didn't you leave the iron on last night? You'd probably say you overlooked it. Well, you sure did, but it wasn't an overlook, it was just an overly forget.

"Another thing: why is your waistline many inches bigger than it was when you were swinging a hoe handle in a cornfield? Well, I'll tell you, you kept in shape then, not from pushing the steam iron, but from pulling weeds and hoeing corn.

"Now your children have flown the roost, and only you and your spouse are here. Enjoy the pretty dresses he buys you, and enjoy the few precious years you both have left. Just remember to always keep your belt pulled down. Don't let it ride up to your chin, like most all old ladies do. For goodness sake keep your lower lip up; most old people drop it so low, you can see their tonsils, and for goodness sake, don't expect sympathy and gifts. You've had enough, give of your time and talents to other people. If you do, that will make you seem younger.

"Look at me now, the misses even hemstitched some designs on me. I got washed this time in Cheer washing powder, and it was much milder than the lye soap your mother washed me in the last time. I was ironed with a steam iron. I had always been ironed with a smoothing iron, heated by a wood fire on the hearth, except in summer when they were heated on the cook stove.

"I got sprayed with Niagara spray starch, and do I look nice on the dining table. I'll be shown to people when they come here. But as old as I'm getting, I might just fall apart any minute.

Hum–I wonder if I really heard the old meal sack talking, or did I fall asleep and dream all this. No, I really think what happened is that I just wanted to tell this little meal sack story and here it is for your reading pleasure. I hope you enjoyed this little fantasy. I told it just as it was told to me; I didn't make up a single word! Honest!

So long!

See ya!

TERRIBLE EXPERIENCE

In early February, I received a phone call from a lady, a descendant of the Craig family, which was well known for its wealth and political power. She was calling for an appointment for a Labor Day family picture. She made sure she had full details about the time, location, and my price for the picture making. Being a Craig, she seemed to think I should spend as much time listening as she wished to spend telling me about the five generations. How Vivian, the fourth generation, had given birth to an eight-pound daughter and she had been named for her great-great-grandmother Carolyn Loraine Craig. Like in any profession, in photography you learn to listen and be polite or you'll soon be out of a job. I was beginning to get jittery for I was supposed to be at a ribbon cutting for the opening of a new K-Mart 20 miles away. I finally managed to interrupt politely and tell her I would be there for the "picture making" on

Labor Day, repeating everything that had been planned. I thanked her for calling and assured her I had already recorded everything in my appointment book.

I rushed out to the new K-Mart to make pictures of the ribbon cutting. It was a cold, clear day. The manager, the mayor of the town, and a few more interested people got their picture made, and the pictures were even published in the town paper.

Time elapsed, spring finally came, then summer. I was mowing the yard one day when my wife came to me and said a woman was on the phone, and it was important that she spoke to me. I cut the lawn mower off and rushed in thinking maybe an unknown rich relative had passed on, leaving me with enough money that I could retire and take my wife and three children places we had never been. We'd go see the Leaning Towers of Pisa. We would go to England and see Queen Elizabeth; I even thought I could pass as her cousin. I was thinking as I entered the house, I would tell the queen I was so proud to visit her and come right out and ask, 'Just why did Charles and Diane separate?' I was going to put it to her straight and direct that mothers-in-laws played a big part in some separations. I finally reached the telephone, and I was so sure a rich unknown relative had died and left me money that I was about to ask how much would be my share.

When I answered the telephone, much to my disappointment, nobody rich had died. Instead, an old lady said, "Please come over to my house as soon as possible." She sounded like a woman in her mid-seventies. I was just sure I would see her husband gasping for a few more good deep breaths. I was in deep sympathy for the poor soul. I asked her for the location, hung up, grabbed my camera, and stepped on the gas.

When I rang the doorbell the Mister and Misses both came forward. I was so sure her sweetie was about to go, it startled me to see him.

The Misses said, "Come in, I have poor Riley on our back porch."

I was sure then that Riley must be a relative maybe smothering to death and they had put him out there for fresh air. As I walked through the house I could see that too much time hadn't been given to house cleaning.

The Misses opened the door and pointing said, "There's poor Riley."

I said, "I don't see anyone."

She looked over her glasses and said, "Can't you see how sick he is? I want his picture made as quickly as possible."

To my surprise there was old Riley barely quaking. Riley turned out to be her pet goose. I angled the camera the best I could at poor Riley; he did act sick. First I made his picture, then one of him and the Misses. She insisted that her honey have his picture taken with Riley. He wasn't too eager to have his made for he wasn't wearing his tie, and his shoes needed polishing. He gave in, of course. After I had finished Riley's picture, the Misses told me she wanted 85 reprints made so she could put them in Christmas cards for her relatives and friends.

After I delivered the pictures to her and got paid in full, I never heard from her again. I just wonder if Riley is still alive. She did say she would let me know when he departed this world. I showed deep sympathy to the old lady, thanked her for the check, (which by the way was quite large), wished them a good day and returned home.

The weekend was quite enjoyable. I hadn't made any appointments because I wanted that time with my wife and kids. We packed the car full of things we needed, such as Tylenol, baby aspirin, Band-Aids, Pepto Bismol, rubbing alcohol, tooth-paste, insect repellent and clothing and loaded the car just as it started raining. We soon ran right out of the rain. We made it fine to the resort where we had reservations already made. The children were perfect little angels; they didn't fight, ate their food, and really enjoyed the fresh country air. We all came back feeling very relaxed. I never dreamed that the weekend with my family could be ruined with Labor Day coming up the next day but maybe being all relaxed was what I needed before making "Family Pictures" at the Craig home.

I got up early, showered, and ate hot biscuits, ham and gravy. I gathered up my camera paraphernalia, tripod, and plenty of film, kissed my wife and kids good-day. Wearing casual clothes like most professional photographers, I headed out to the elaborate home of Mr. and Mrs. Craig. They were the great-great grandmother and grandfather of the new baby. As I drove up I was greeted graciously by a number of relatives, some in full suits, some in sport clothes and sneakers. Mr. and Mrs. Craig were dressed to perfection, although Mrs. Craig had overdone it with jewelry. She seemed to want everybody to see all the pretty rings, bracelets, and ear screws she had. They offered me a glass of lemonade and a big chunk of coconut cake. I thanked them politely and bragged on the cake and lemonade.

I had promised Gaygene I would try to be back in probably an hour and half, but it certainly didn't work out that way. Everyone seemed to be anxious to get in order at the selected spot they had chosen to have the pictures made. The Craig home was just beautiful, the landscape and scenery was a picture within itself, rolling hills distant mountains, and flowers blooming as if it were early spring. The grounds were well groomed by a professional gardener. The beauty of it, however, was blocked by the expensive cars parked all around.

The cars were Cadillacs, Lincolns, expensive vans, all with out-of-state licenses, one Harley Davidson motorcycle, and granddaddy Craig's 4-wheel-drive Jeep parked out front. He kept his Rolls Royce parked in his garage. He loved it so much he didn't want anything touching it.

At last I got to set up my equipment for the family to assemble. I knew well how to arrange people for a group picture. Grandpa and Grandma were supposed to be seated on the chairs, with small children beside them sitting on the ground. Then came the adults, with whom I thought I had done an excellent job, but there was one thing I had left unnoticed: the mother Zella with the fifth-generation baby, which she named for her great-great-grandmother Carolyn Loraine. I guess she might have thought giving her baby Grandmother's name might put her first or second in their will. Anyway, I crowded them in where baby Carolyn was sure to be seen. I was almost ready to make the first snap when Grandmother had to be excused. Grandpa was already getting a little touchy and he remarked, "I told her not to be drinking so much tea." Those who knew Grandma knew she could care less what the old man said. She waddled off to the bathroom and was gone longer than Grandfather could account for, so he took off after her. They never stayed put out at each other very long. After seating them I was anxious to get moving, until Grandmother said, "Oh dear me. Look at Mr. Craig's hair–he must have it combed." The best I could count hurriedly he had perhaps two dozens strands of hair, and now they were all out of place.

"Jeff!" Grandmother spoke out, "Run to the house and get your grandfather's comb. It's lying on the dresser in our room. Now hurry ,Jeff, before everybody loses their smiles." Jeff left running; he was nine years old and could run like a deer. Everyone was hoping he'd hurry back real soon. But minutes passed and Jeff didn't return. Finally Jeff's father got disgusted waiting for him and took off to the house, finding Jeff involved in watching a rodeo on television. He yanked poor Jeff up by the hair on his head and got Grandpa's comb and did a good job arranging the two dozen hairs.

I politely asked in a jovial manner, "Are we ready? Everyone answered yes with the exception of Jennifer and little Sue who had gotten so tickled at Jeff's little fit he had just pulled that they were unable to calm down. Their mothers were losing their good graces and bopped their little girls on the bottoms, which upset the grandmothers, and I thought for a while there might be a free-for-all. When calmness came over the crowds, I asked for the fifteenth time, "Are we ready?" Zella raised her hand and asked to be excused; she said, "I do believe baby Carolyn needs a change." Off she went, hurrying as fast as she could walk, carrying an eight-month-old baby. Before she could get back, Mrs. Craig remembered she wanted to wear her heart necklace that Mr. Craig gave her the night he proposed, such a tender moment that she had relived it many times.

She had already forgotten about having a few unpleasant words with him only minutes before. This time her daughter Jane went for the necklace, for Grandmother had shown her where she kept it hidden. It was an expensive piece of jewelry, a big 14-karat-gold heart on a chain, and she had in it Mr. Craig's picture, with lots of hair on his head. Mr. Craig never told Mrs. Craig that he had to borrow money from his old bachelor Uncle Henry to pay for it. Neither did she know that he never paid it back. Well, Uncle Henry passed on before Mr. Craig hit oil, and how can he pay it back now? I really can't figure that one out. Jane got back, put the necklace on Grandmother's wrinkled neck, and took her place in the group.

"Now, are we ready?" I asked. Just as everyone grinned, up a puff of wind came and sent poor Opal's wig flying through the air. She didn't have much more hair than her poor father. Opal's sweetheart of 20 years raced after the wig, but just as he would be able to pounce upon it, a friendly little breeze would yank it up and take it a little further. Finally luck came to his rescue. He put his big foot on the wig and crushed it into the ground. Opal was so embarrassed over the ordeal, for no one had ever seen Opal's bare head, not even Oliver, her beloved friend. She grabbed the wig out of Oliver's hands, and she was so embarrassed she put it on backward, and everyone's grins froze.

I called for their attention again, and as I was just ready to mash the button poor Uncle Glenn sneezed and out popped his upper plate. Harriet his wife was so irritated with waiting, she let poor Glenn have it, accusing him of not putting his hand over his mouth while sneezing. Poor hen-pecked Glenn grabbed his teeth, which almost landed in something nasty, and put them in his mouth, borrowed a grin from his cousin, and posed. Harriet scolded poor Glenn in such a rip roaring tone of voice that baby Carolyn got scared and cried her lungs out for awhile.

Grandmother asked to say something and she did; she said it loud and clear: "If I hear one more word out of any of you, we'll have a new will made tomorrow. Now everybody smile like nothing has happened." Well, I'll tell you that was the wisest thing I had heard all day. Everybody was trying to smile and the most disgusted ones put their fingers in the corners of their mouths, to force a smile.

It didn't take me long to take a roll of film for the Craig family. I soon gathered up my paraphernalia and started home, that is after every one had told me how many 10 x 12's they wanted. Poor Opal asked for some, but I didn't dare tell her she had put her wig on backward. Maybe she'll look like she's goin' instead of comin'.

I rushed home, exhausted to my bones. Gaygene had a delicious dinner ready and I ate too much. After telling her about my experience and playing with the kids a while, I took a hot shower and three nerve pills and went to sleep at three o'clock the next morning.

Just wait until they get their bill for the pictures. Mr. Craig has oil wells, so he shouldn't feel too bad. Got to go make a picture of a raccoon in a garbage pail.

So long!

See ya!

DRINK
Coca-Cola
SAM J. JO
CAVALIER
DRINK
Dr Pepper

THE MAGIC ROOSTER

There has been magic in the hearts and minds of children since the beginning of time, but I wonder if there has ever been a magic rooster like mine. I'm not sure this one is magic, but I do know I bought more with him than any other person this side of the Mason-Dixon line could have bought. This is a true story. If you have any doubts, my four sisters will vouch for me.

My three older sisters were struggling for an education. By struggling I don't necessarily mean having to study hard for good grades, but rather, the way they had to travel to school. There were no school buses to catch. My parents didn't have a car to take them. Walking was the only way. They got up early, ate a hot breakfast of ham, bacon or sausage, gravy, molasses and home–made churned butter on hot biscuits, right from the oven. After breakfast they packed their lunches which usually consisted of jellies, jams, apple butter, ham, or sausage on biscuits with a slice of cake or a piece of apple pie. In winter heavy coats, toboggans, high-topped shoes, and cotton stockings were needed for the long two-mile walk to the school that had only one teacher for all eight grades. Going to and from school they walked rocks to cross the creeks – sometimes missing a rock and ending up with wet feet. The roads weren't even graveled, so they were plenty muddy in the rainy weather and so were everyone's shoes.

I was a pre-schooler trying to be a good girl. That is, when I was in my mother's sight. It was just impossible to be a good girl all the time. One thing is for sure; I liked money and liked to hear the pennies and nickels clank as I put them in my little tin bank. My first experience with making money was when my two older sisters offered to give me one of their prized chickens, if I would feed their chickens while they were at school. They had only one flock which had hatched off earlier in the summer. I don't know if they felt sorry for me when they gave me such an wonderful opportunity to make big money or whether they just wanted their chickens fed.

They also gave me a little game rooster. I thought he was cute. Maybe they wanted to keep the pullets so they could sell eggs. That was quite a job for a little four-year-old girl, but even then I guess money talked. I fed the chickens daily and watched my little game cock grow.

I had plenty of time to dream about the future. I would buy Mama a new dress, Papa a new shirt, a little pedal car so I could go to town, which was 12 or 15 miles from where we lived, something for my baby sister, and gifts for my three older sisters. Oh, yes, I must get Grandma and Aunt Mandy something. At that time I had a heart of gold. My rooster would have to be magic to buy everything.

After waiting a long time, Mama finally siad my rooster was big enough to sell. Mama caught him and tied his legs together so he couldn't fly out of her market basket. She made sure I was clean and my hair was combed. We made the two mile walk to the store without any problems. Ike, the owner and operator of Peanut's Store, greeted us. He laid my little rooster on the scales but didn't tell me how much he weighed. It really didn't matter because I couldn't multiply pounds and dollars anyway.

As Ike started to put the poor thing in a pen, where he kept chickens aftere he bought them, the little cock got loose and ran right through Long Creek which was deep and cold. Nolan Ottinger, a young man who just happened to be at the store, and Ike ran through the creek and caught that little rooster just as he was crowing his big hallelujah for having escaped. After returning with the rooster, they teased me by saying they would have to have the price of the rooster for catching him and getting all wet. I don't reckon I fainted, but I'll bet I turned purple from such a shock. Thankfully, they were just teasing.

Ike started figuring how much he owed me. I'm not sure how much it was, but Mama said I had enough rooster money to buy material for a dress for myself. But what about all the other gifts I had planned to buy? I had been too extravagant in my planning. While looking over the beautiful bolts of gingham and percale, I became a little selfish. I decided on the lavendar and green gingham. Ike measured it off the bolt and figured the price.

I had one nickel left – and a buffalo nickel at that! While trying to decide if I should save my nickel or buy candy for my sisters, I looked up and right in front of my eyes was the glass case where Ike kept his candy. The coconut balls in white, pink, yellow, and chocolate coverings caught my eye. The buffalo nickel was back in his possession, and I believe he gave me a real good bargain on the candy deal. After Mama and I got home, I shared my candy with my sisters, Papa, and Mama. We even had more than one piece around. It had been a wonderful day!

Even though the rooster really wasn't magic, I had enjoyed planning to buy for others. Mama made my dress, and I'm sure I wore it as long as I could breathe in it. Seventy one years later, I have a vivid picture in my mind of the little game rooster, Ike, Nolan, coconut candy, and my pretty lavendar and green checked dress.

So Long!

See ya!

RECORD CROWD ATTENDS COUNTY FAIR

The September weather was ideal for the annual country fair. All the people that had any talent participated in it, from quilting quilts to yodeling and lots of crafts and activities between. There were prizes for the prettiest baby and the best cakes and pies. People started arriving early with their prized exhibits and wearing their Sunday go-to-meeting clothes. Even old man Clifford Warder wore the new shirt that his son had given him for Christmas two years ago. Everybody said he just wore it because he knew Flossie Mae Garber would be there and he had been trying to cut around her ever since his wife Mayme had died three years before.

Everybody knew Flossie Mae (being an old maid) was playing it cool, but everybody also knew she liked him from the way she cut her eyes around at him.

Soon the fairground was filled to capacity. Frank Jacks was the coordinator and he was feeling his oats. He was a fat, rolly-polly fellow and seemed to think he owned the full contents–not only the fair, but the whole county. He was quite a lady's man and tried hard to have possession of as many as would look in his direction, especially Madge Sane. She was pretty and had a figure that would make a statue raise up and whistle. He wasn't her type, for she liked younger men, especially if they had a pretty car. In fact, Henry Gregg caught Madge and Grover Ayres behind the old garage at the edge of the fair ground, and he wouldn't tell anyone what went on. They could have been smoking marijuana.

Madge was one of these women that dressed to get whistles and she knew how to twist her hips and manipulate and control any desires she might arouse, and she usually did. Being the prettiest girl in the neighborhood gave her control over whatever she desired.

Another important character in my story is poor Lucy Goins, who was a homely old spinster who tended to her own business, except at times when she saw things differently. Then she might do a little nose poking. She couldn't understand why Madge wore tight-fitting skirts and blouses with low necks and long dangling ear screws, and she never liked the way Madge wore her hair. Then there was her makeup. Madge always wore too much in Lucy's way of seeing things. Maybe it all boiled down to a little bit of jealousy. Lucy always seemed to have her eyes on Grover and often made him cakes and pies. That was the old way of gaining a husband, by feeding the brute, or that was what Grandma told her and she thought what Grandma said was law and gospel. That wasn't exactly what Grover considered in a woman. Grover was interested in–well, you know!

Frank Kelley was asked to be the baking judge. He was a big husky man with a deep, loud voice that could be heard almost to the county line. All the women were busy uncovering the cakes as that was to be the first contest. There was Molly's big four-layer yellow cake with caramel frosting on it. Jessie's was a white Lady Baltimore cake; the recipe had been in the family since the turn of the century. She had it decorated in pink and white frosting and she knew she would get the blue ribbon for sure. Poor Alice didn't get to first base with hers, for she forgot to put sugar in it. Then there was Clara's cake. She turned her back on Johnny, her three-year-old son, and he poured half a bottle of garlic powder in the dough. Poor Clara had a bad cold and couldn't smell it. There were more cakes, but Madge's was last.

It was a banana cake, with the layers sliding right and left. The icing was soft and runny. Frank was doing right well sampling the cakes until he started looking a little pale. All of a sudden he turned the job over to Grover while he rushed off to the little boys' room. He had eaten too many green apples the day before.

Grover was pleased to get to finish the job as Madge's cake was yet to be judged. After tasting each one of the cakes and reaching the last one, which just happened to be Madge's, he ate a big bite, belched real loud, and made the decision. After discussing it with Frank Jacks, he took the microphone and gave the report.

The white ribbon goes to Edna Lane, the red one to Gona Fine, and the blue ribbon to our own Madge Sane. That was more than poor Lucy could endure. She flew into Madge like a chicken on a June bug. Poor Madge looked almost as homely as Lucy by the time the deputy stepped between and stopped the fight. Lucy gave the deputy her butterscotch pie and stopped a law suit.

Herman Luttrell got so tickled at the fight he swallowed a big cud of tobacco and got so sick he turned purple. Words came out of his mouth that could never be printed and Angeline heard it all and got so tickled she wet her pants.

Next came the judging of the quilts. There were Lone Stars, Double Wedding Rings, Nine Diamonds, Trip Around the World, Odd Fellows and many more to be chosen. Gertrude Neas had the prettiest one there to the eyes of most all the women. Bonnie Fields was a very jealous woman, as everybody knew, and she was around eyeing and envying all the pretty art work. She was slurping a glass of grape Kool-Aid and everybody thought she did it on purpose when she accidentally spilled the stuff on Gertrude's beautiful quilt. Poor

Gertrude almost fainted and after she came to, it was overheard that she threatened to put Purex in Bonnie's cistern.

Next came the judging of the cattle and chickens. Gomer Waddell had a pretty game rooster that he was almost sure would take the blue ribbon. Poor Gomer! He was fixing to groom the strutting little cock up a bit and by queer fate the little rascal escaped and poor Gomer ran after him, tripping on his shoe laces.

He fell to the ground and got mud all over the brand new white shirt he had meant to wear to church on Sunday. Gomer's wife Monnie saw it all and even though she had her pink silk dress on and her pocket book under her arm and was carrying her bright blue umbrella and wearing her spiked high heel shoes, she forgot it all and took after the little cock, running through briers and tearing her Sunday silk stockings. They finally caught him just as he started to fly across the fence that surrounded a pond.

Well, it all paid off. Gomer got the blue ribbon. But they had to stay out of church the next day because Gomer's white shirt was muddy and Monnie had ruined her silk stockings. This all happened while poor old lady Hawkings was standing off to herself, scratching where it itched. She had gone blackberry picking the day before and got more chiggers than she did berries.

Next came the baby-judging contest. Grover was so full of cake sampling that he almost ignored the babies. Maybe it was because he couldn't flirt with them. Anyway, Garry and Fern Fann's baby won the blue ribbon, even if he did look like Abe Lincoln.

Finally, the yodeling contest came last, but not least. Dozens tried out for it, but what startled the crowd was when Virginia Cole started yodeling, which she did quite often. She yodeled so loud that the cakes started sliding off the bench they were on. One slid on old lady Bertha's lap and ruined the new apron that she had worked hard at putting lace and appliqué on.

Seems like this is all that happened this year at the fair worth writing about. With the folks that live here to talk about, I'm sure that next year will be even more interesting. Friendsville is a soap opera every day!

So long!

See ya!

MOTORCYCLE ROSE

She was known as Rosie to all her friends and acquaintances and even others who cared less about knowing her at all. She was a tall muscular woman with dark brown hair and eyes that could cut through steel. She was not a lovable person but all who knew her could identify her as a person who would go beyond expectations to accommodate you.

Rosie's greatest desires were to own and operate a Harley Davidson motorcycle and to have full possession of her true love, Frank Peters. He was not a very handsome man at all, very tall and clumsy with shoulder length bright red hair which he never kept groomed. In fact, there wasn't anything about him that showed any sign of good grooming. Inside his rough exterior, though, he had a heart of gold, or, at least a silver one.

Rose and Frank were walking one Sunday afternoon in a pasture where daisies grew. Rose loved everything pertaining to fortune telling or what the future had in store for her. When she saw the daisies, she grabbed one of the flowers and told Frank she was going to see if he loved her. She started plucking a petal at a time saying, "He loves me, he loves me not." As she plucked the last one, it ended in "he loves me not." Rosie had a way of temperamental pouting. She believed in any superstition she heard.

She started shaking her arms and head and accused poor Frank of just dragging her on. When Frank could get a word in, he tried to explain that daisies didn't always prove the full meaning of what people tried to make them do. Poor Frank, after taking much abuse, finally persuaded her to try another. This time it came out just right and then she believed it.

After the second daisy experience, Rose renewed her hope that her Aunt Rhoda would soon kick the bucket and her part of the estate would be enough to buy the cycle and get her wedding gown and veil. Many nights she had lain awake and planned for that fortunate time.

Things just didn't turn out that well for Rosie. Aunt Rhoda made a turn for the better and was soon up and about. Rose sent her a real pretty "Get Well" card with a mushy verse on it that made Aunt Rhoda think she was her very special aunt. Poor Rhoda! If she had known Rose's thoughts she would never left her name in her will.

Days, months, and seasons passed and Aunt Rhoda was doing just splendidly. Rose was chewing her fingernails and popping her gum. That is, she would pop her gum when Frank had money to buy her a pack.

Things usually happen when least expected. Rose and Frank were making big plans to go with a group on a hiking trip to the Smokies for two days. Everything was in order. Rose was taking her dandruff shampoo and a bottle of turpentine to keep chiggers off. Frank put his corn and bunion medicine in the satchel and sneaked rub-on stuff in for his arthritis that Rose didn't know about. Just as everyone was ready to start, Rose saw little Roscoe running down the road waving his arms and yelling, "Wait, wait!"

After getting to the stopping point he was so near out of breath all he could say was "Aunt Rhoda." Rose heard him and dollar marks started flying before her eyes. And she jumped, thinking a motorcycle was coming down from above. After getting over the excitement that poor Rhoda had finally died, she put on such an act that most anyone would have thought she really loved Aunt Rhoda instead of her money. Frank tried to console her. He took his hat off and fanned her with all that his big muscles would put out. Rosie put on a fake faint. Claude and Vera rushed to the creek with a bucket, filled it, and drenched her with cold water. That stopped the trip for Rose and Frank but it put a sparkle in Rose's eyes no one had ever seen before.

Weeks passed and finally the day came for the reading of the will. All brothers and sisters and their sons and daughters and even some supposedly disinterested people came for curiosity's sake. They were just anxious to know how much Rose would rake in.

Well, Rose's dream came true. She got enough money to buy her a brand new Harley Davidson motorcycle, a pretty white dress and a veil with a thousand and six sequins on it, a new bottle of dandruff shampoo, an imitation diamond ring and a whole box of cigars for Frank.

Rose could hardly wait for her new Harley-Davidson. She could hear that brrr-brr, brrr -ing in her ears. Now she must learn to drive it. She had never learned to ride a tricycle, much less a motorcycle!

That great day finally came! Sitting out front, under the shade of the old oak tree, was Rose's beautiful black and red set of wheels. Frank came over and looked it over with envious eyes, then all the neighbors came for the first peek of the priceless vehicle.

Time was wasting. Rose could not keep herself off it any longer. She felt that she could handle it if anyone else could. But I forgot; she had some money left from buying the other things mentioned earlier, so she bought two helmets, two pairs of motorcycle boots, two pairs of goggles, two leather jackets and twelve pairs of sweat-resistant socks for Frank, for she said she couldn't stand to smell stinking feet.

Rose wanted Frank to go with her on her first experimental trip, but being chicken and not wanting to run the risk of getting killed, he claimed to have backache and sat in the shade until Rose got back. All the neighbors knew she was making her first triumphant trip down the road and they fastened their kids up tight inside their houses. Even the adults stood breathless on their porches, while Jake Emory and Sid Miles climbed a tree to be safe. Rose was keeping the monster very well under control until she looked in the side mirror to see just how lovely she looked. Then she lost control and almost hit the tree Jake and Sid were hiding in. Jake was so scared he opened his mouth and lost his partial plate and Sid jerked his head back and caught his glasses in a limb and broke a side piece off.

After getting everything under control and learning to handle the cycle professionally, Rose started making plans for the wedding. It was plain for people to see that the motorcycle came first and then the wedding. Poor Frank, unable to see an inch before his eyes, accepted her proposal for marriage. Everything was in top-notch order. Daddy and Mama put out some of Aunt Rhoda's money on the wedding just to kind of show off. Daddy bought a new suit and

Mama bought herself a real fancy dress with ruffles and bows and even got her hair fixed at the Beauty Salon. They had a big cake and decorated it like a motorcycle.

Frank had bought himself a new suit with the money he had saved from washing cars last summer at the world's fair.

Everything went well at the wedding. The preacher preached on smoking and abortion. He finally quit before the ice all melted in the punch.

After being showered with rice and bird seed, Rose and Frank climbed on that shiny Harley Davidson motorcycle. Rose was happy for the first time in her life. The sun was shining and the sequins in her veil sparkled until the guests watching had to put their colored glasses on to watch them as they went racing down the road with Rose in her wedding gown and veil flying at half mast. They turned the curve, and no one has ever seen them since.

A salesman from Alaska came by one day and made mention of Rose and Frank and how they had put a trailer to their Harley Davidson cycle for their two sets of triplets to ride in. Everybody back home came to the conclusion it must be them, for the salesman mentioned that one set of triplets had red hair and the other set had black.

Good luck and blessings, Rose and Frank. We think you have done real well. But I wonder, did any of Rose's sequins came off riding all that distance

So long!

See ya!

CARL BEAN

VERONICA, HER VIOLIN AND VERNON.

Because of the kind of violinist that she was, Veronica's manager Vernon kept bookings months ahead of time. She was an avid musician, and she could play classical, bluegrass, gospel or anything pertaining to music.

Veronica loved her violin almost as much as she did Vernon. Being Vernonica's manager gave Vernon the chance of being with her every minute she would allow him.

There was something about the way Veronica played the violin that enchanted everyone, whereever she might be. Always encores, and more encores. She could make the roughest, toughest men cry that hadn't cried since their mothers smacked their hands when they put them in the brown sugar jars as little boys. Uncontrollable tears streamed down their hairy faces as they listened in awe. She could make the violin talk. Each note spoke the words of the song she was playing.

Seats were sold out months before the scheduled time. It was told by news reporters that preachers were envious of her, and jealousy spread like wild fire when she would perform in churches. The melody she could get from an old gospel song would bring hardshell sinners to the front for confession. That was when the preachers could have broken the bow and torn the strings off her violin. The reason for the jealousy was that as many times the preachers had pleaded for the sinners to repent, they were never able to touch them like Veronica and her violin could.

Had it not been for Veronica's talent, she could never have had the popularity she was graced with. She loved her bubble gum and kept time by popping it, often blowing bubbles. Not only that, but she was uncouth. She refused to practice her manners. Her mother tried hard to teach her manners, but Veronica thought they were for other people.

Many people thought she'd step on their toes just to see them flinch. Many times she coughed in people's faces. If she had to burp, she burped, regardless of how loud it might sound. The words excuse me or pardon me were never used. If she sneezed she never bothered to cover her mouth.

When she was younger she had fallen off a horse and lost three front teeth, which had to be replaced with partials. One day while she was performing, she had a sneezing spell, and out popped her partial, falling on the stage where hundreds of people saw it. For once Veronica was embarrassed. Vernon, being the good guy he was, hastily grabbed the partial up, swiped a handkerchief over it, and gave it back to her. She shortened the music, left the stage, put it back in her mouth, and came back to play some more.

She was very bad at interrupting people when they were talking. People wondered if she thought she should have the floor at all times. If food didn't taste to suit her, Veronica wouldn't hesitate in telling the hostess what she thought about it and would send it back and ask for a clean plate. Also, she always scratched where it itched. Poor Vernon, with all his politeness and all the love he had for her, would sometimes see daggers and would almost wish he had one to use on her.

Finally the day came when she was performing at the White House for the President, and like all others he was more than impressed with her beautiful playing. Just as he started to shake her hand and congratulate her, she let out a big burp. Being as the burp was so unexpected, the President was embarrassed to the point that he started laughing and you know how his face turns red when he laughs. That really put her where she belonged, and for once in her life she asked to be excused. The President accepted the apology.

On the way back from D.C. Vernon asked her why she did things like that when she was so popular with her musical entertainment. Veronica was silent for a while and broke into tears, asking herself "Why do I do things like that?" It came to her at last. When she was growing up, her mother tried very hard to teach her manners, and being the stubborn child she was, it all boiled down to resentment of her mother.

Vernon told her how very much he loved her and had wanted to propose to her all through the years. "But," he said, "I have been waiting for you to see yourself as others see you, and today you saw through the eyes of the most powerful man in the nation. He had to laugh at you to wake you up." Then came the question: "Veronica, will you marry me?" Without hesitation, she answered with a quick, "Yes."

After all those years of stubborn living, Veronica apologized to her mother, and like all mothers will do, she accepted the apology and started helping with plans for their wedding. The wedding was a big affair with all her friends and big numbers of acquaintances attending. Veronica continued with her concerts but it was a different Veronica. They traveled for quite some time and, taking some time off, Veronica presented Vernon with a little daughter. And to help make things better for Mom, they named her little girl after her mother, which made Mom happy, and Granddaddy was well pleased too.

Hope the baby doesn't build up resentment against VeronicaWhen the baby burped in public, Veronica pitched a fit. Maybe the baby will quit impolite things quicker than Veronica did. I sure hope so.

Got to turn T. V. on and watch "Wheel of Fortune."

So long!

See ya!

A CAR GRAVEYARD

I don't know why I chose a night like that to pay a visit to a car graveyard. If you've never been to one, take my advice and stay home. The moon was casting shadows over the hillside, and down in the low-lying land numbers of wrecked cars lay helpless. The wind was making dreadful sounds, as if to tell me to not go any farther. Being a big coward afraid of my own shadow, I wondered why I had come to such a ghostly place as this. Hesitating, I was almost at the point of returning to my car. But, something within me seemed to urge me on, forced me to take another step, though I sometimes slid back two. I was becoming very exhausted from fright and heart palpitation, and maybe picking my feet up a little too fast. Suddenly I heard the mournful sounds of broken down vehicles.

I stopped to catch my breath and try to calm my nerves. I leaned against a 1981 black Lincoln, thinking I heard voices. I cried out, "Hello, Mr. Lincoln," and a deep voice answered "Hello." I asked, "Why are you here?"

Answering in a deep car voice, he said, "I'm here because my owner did it to me. Look how my doors are caved in, my windows are broken out, and my insides are all smashed. But the sad story I have to endure is, that my owner had too much to drink, his wife begged him to let her drive home, but being drunk and stubborn he refused to let her. They had their three children with them, and as they went around the last bad curve to home, he pulled too far to the left, and rolled down a steep hill. I shiver all over when I think of hearing the screaming children. Suddenly everything became quiet. An ambulance came and took two of the children away. They died. Later on a wrecker came and pulled me up the incline. I overheard my owner say something I'll remember until all my parts rust away. He said, "If I could only call back yesterday, I would be playing ball with my sons instead of drinking whisky. My lesson has been learned, but like so many people, I learned it too late." Mr. Lincoln then told me to go talk to his neighbors, for they too, could tell me hair-raising stories.

Trudging along hypnotized at what I was hearing, I suddenly came to a halt. Right before my eyes was a battered, caved-in 1993 red Porsche with silver trim. I knocked on the door and a voice cried out saying, "I'd rather not be bothered right now." Scared out of my wits at hearing cars talk, I managed to get words out, saying, "I only wanted to get a report on your accident, Mr. Porsche." Before he could answer, a swarm of bats flew over me, and a hooting owl tried his best at finishing me off with his scary sounds. By then Mr. Porsche changed his mind and started telling me his story. My fear suddenly changed to laughter, so listen and you'll laugh too.

Mr. Porsche said, "This accident happened one Saturday afternoon when my owner, the Reverend Grover Myers, got a telephone call early Saturday morning from a dear member of his church. Mrs. Carrie Duffey said one of her dear aunts had taken very ill and her husband was out of town and she was too shaken up to drive. Grover was much concerned and explained to his dearly beloved wife how he felt that he should take her, since Mrs. Duffey was such a devoted Christian, which she showed everyone every Sunday with her shouts. Mrs. Myers thought it a good idea for Grover to take her and even suggested she go along. But the foxy Rev. Grover convinced her the trip would be long and tiresome.

Being the good trustful soul she was, she stayed home. Which was exactly what the Reverend wanted." Rushing around getting properly dressed, he was heard whistling songs that were popular when he was a teenager. What was it all about? Well, things had been happening in the church in closed rooms that no one ever suspected. Mrs. Duffey usually had something to take to the church, or a job needed to be done, that only she could do. Well, Mr. Duffey and Mrs. Myers lived in the dark like most all the other church people."

"Rev. Myers picked Carrie up, wearing a smile from ear to ear, and at the same time Carrie wasn't doing any loud bawling. As they were driving along, things began to get a little mushy (that is if you could ever believe a preacher doing a thing like that) and Grover let his emotions run wild and forgot about being a preacher. He pulled off the side of a road and cut my motor off, and they were soon in each others arms and . . . By then a police car pulled up behind them and opened up his siren, almost ruining everything, But since Grover was reliving his teenage years, he started up my motor and peeled out, slinging gravel high in the sky. He was so excited he ran a stop sign. An on-coming truck plowed right into me, and you see what happened. Grover was able to get me back home, and luckily Grover and Carrie only got minor injuries and were stiff for several days. The preacher stood in the pulpit the next day and, well, he kind of lied and said they got on the wrong road when the accident happened. No one doubted the story except for one person. Custodians see and hear a lot, and that's just what happened. Mrs. Weems the custodian came out and looked me over, and she told me what went on behind closed church doors and then I returned the favor and told her what I just told you. "

The story I heard got me over my scare and I went on. Here was a battered-up 1975 green Oldsmobile. I could see a good story there, so I leaned my shoulder against a door and called, "Wake up in there!" and I heard the horn blow. "What do you want?" a voice called, "Are you after some of my good parts? Just like others, they come here stripping off all my parts that can be used again. Well, I'll tell you, I don't like it. I was taken good care of by two good ladies. I was kept dry in a garage, was washed and vacuumed regularly. Never driven over 45 miles an hour, I got oil changes regularly, and check ups when needed."

"Finally my owners got too old to drive and their favorite nephew inherited me. What else could I expect from a 16-year-old boy? He and three other boys were trying me out and what do you think happened? I got wrapped around a telephone pole. Luckily the boys were unhurt. But I'm paying for it, parked in a lonely car graveyard."

The moon was covered with clouds and a mournful sound could be heard throughout the lonely auto yard. I made one last stop. I was standing beside a beautiful 1995 white Cadillac which had every extra that could be put on a car. I called out, "Hey, Mr. Cadillac, why are you here in a wrecked car lot? You don't have a scar on you."

Mr. Cadillac said, " Come around on the other side, then you'll see why I'm here." I did as he suggested and I saw what had happened: the whole passenger side was completely caved in. I said, "Mr. Cadillac, what in the world happened?" Mr. Cadillac said, "Well, I don't like to tell tales, but if Glenn hadn't been trying to show off it never would have happened. He was driving entirely too fast and hit the side of a building. Thanks for seat belts or he would have been killed. Debbie, his wife, was home sick with the flu or she would have been killed. Hope he learned his lesson well. By the way, he's driving a car he bought on credit at a used car lot. A bird never comes down until it's flown too high. Do you know what I mean?"

It's coming daylight I must get out of here. But, I do know what the old Cadillac meant. I'll be careful so my car won't end up in the car graveyard telling private stuff to anyone who might be drawn there, just as I was that night.

So long!

See ya!

NO TIME FOR THE BRIDE AND GROOM

The wedding date was drawing near. Plans had been underway for months. Faye Broyles, Glenn's mother, and Bernice Hartley, Joy's mother, were trying to out-do each other. Both mothers fully intended to be the best dressed, have the latest hair style, and wear the most fashionable shoes and accessories.

Glenn and Joy were the Broyles' and Hartley's babies. Even though Faye and Burnice had already seen their other sons and daughters marry, it didn't keep them from being heartbroken at having to give their babies up.

Faye and Lester were determined to have a better rehearsal dinner than Bernice and Clyde had for Robert, their son. On the other hand, Bernice and

Clyde had every intention of doing more for Joy than Faye and Lester had done for their daughter, Julia. They were making plans for one of the most elaborate weddings that Friendsville had ever seen. The wedding invitations had Joy's and Glenn's pictures on them engraved in silver.

No one had ever heard of so many showers and luncheons given to one person. This made Bernice feel very important for she very well remembered that Julia, Faye's daughter, didn't have nearly so many. Both families trying to outdo each other helped to make the stock market rise. Neither family would ever admit it, but they weren't exactly in favor of the marriage. Like many parents, each one thought the other one wasn't good enough for their baby.

As far as Joy and Glen were concerned they would have settled for a quiet wedding in the church parsonage. But that wasn't Faye's and Bernice's wishes for they wanted big stuff–and got it.

For the wedding Bernice chose an off-the-shoulder pale pink chiffon crepe trimmed in the same shade of lace. She had it styled in Paris. She felt like Faye would have no way of being dressed better than she. In the meantime, Faye was having her dress made by one of the most popular seamstresses in America. It was said that this seamstress had taken lessons from Jacquiline Kennedy's seamstress. Her dress was imported pale blue tulle, lined in matching pure silk. The skirt was full and long with a matching sash. It was tied in the back in a large bow. The men chose black tuxedoes with black striped pants and black bow ties.

The banquet room in the Colonial Hotel was set for the rehearsal dinner. Every fancy dish Faye had ever heard of she had the chefs prepare. Drinks of any choice were available. The room was decorated in extravagant style. The tables were covered in pink satin overlaid in expensive lace. A popular band furnished music while the guests ate.

Saturday, May 16, was the day two people would be joined together in wedlock. Bernice and Clyde had worked endlessly preparing for the occasion.

Musical bows in pale pink were placed at the side of the seats, and as the guests were seated the bows played a soft wedding tune.

The bridesmaids wore pale green silk dresses with matching hair bows and carried nosegays of white gardenias. The matron of honor wore a deep shade of green silk and carried a bouquet of baby pink roses.

As the bride, attended by her father, entered the sanctuary, a violinist played "To You I Give My Love" while a college friend of Joy's sang. Bernice and Faye blinked back tears while some ran down their faces, smudging the expensive make-up the beauticians had so carefully put on them. If Clyde and Lester would have had makup on, I'm sure it might have been smeared too. When the preacher asked, "Who gives this woman away?" Clyde replied in a choked voice, "Her mother and I," and kissed Joy. He then took his seat by Bernice.

Bernice did outdo Faye: the wedding reception was far above the rehearsal dinner, if that was possible. The food was beyond reason, and the caterers were dressed as if they belonged to the wedding party. Since they were high-class caterers, not one mistake was made. The food was delicious and there was plenty of it.

Joy's gown was made from soft white material. The skirt was trimmed in ruffles with a small edging around each ruffle. The waist was fitted and had a scooped, rounded neckline and puffed short sleeves. She wore a single strand of pearls around her neck that Glenn had given her for a graduation gift in high school. Her engagement ring was a two-karat round setting with much sparkle to it.

The afternoon soon passed and Joy and Glenn were ready to leave for their honeymoon, dressed in navy suits. Joy wore a corsage of baby's breath and pink rose buds. Before they left, they made the dreadful mistake of telling their parents where they were going. Sneaky as Faye was, she had nosed in and found their reservations were at a hotel in Spartinburg, South Carolina. She had even called the hotel and gotten their room number and telephone number. She had a way of getting information from people, even if they weren't supposed to tell. Pretending she cared for Bernice and Clyde, she gave them the location and telephone number.

It was getting late when Joy and Glenn arrived at the hotel. After checking in and putting a "Do not disturb" marker on their door, they unpacked and relaxed, but not for long. The telephone rang, and it was dear old mom. Glenn answered, saying, "Yes mom, this is Glenn. Yes, we arrived safely. No, we haven't eaten. We aren't hungry, and after all, we just got here. Thanks for calling, mom."

After they cooled down from the call and got a little intimate, another call came in, this time from Joy's mom. Bernice said, "Faye called and told us you were there and had arrived safely. Dad and I just wanted to call and congratulate you both. We're so proud of both of you and we wish you well." It was all they could do to keep from hanging up. Finally Clyde and Bernice told them how much they loved them, and how much they'd miss them and hung up. Bernice called Faye and told her they had called, and all about the conversation. Faye wanted to be the last caller and called again. By now Joy and Glenn were becoming very annoyed. Faye could be very lovable when she wanted to be, especially when she was making a telephone call. She asked in a very sweet voice, "Is this Glenn Broyles?" Glenn came very near saying no, it's Santa Claus, but he didn't; he said, "Yes, mom. This is Glenn Broyles. What do you want this time?" Faye knew by the tone of his voice he had all the telephone calls he could endure for the day. "Oh," said Faye, "I just wondered if you thought to bring your new pajamas I bought for you to take with you?"

"How do I know?" Glenn answered shortly. You haven't given me time to check," and he hung up. Joy and Glenn hoped that would be the last call for the night. They hoped wrong, for Faye called Bernice and told her Glenn seemed very annoyed and she couldn't understand why. Bernice became very worried that Glenn and Joy might be having problems, and she felt like she could never go to sleep until she was sure they were all right.

The telephone rang again! It was spoiling everything. This time Joy answered, "Hello, mom. Yes, we're fine. Why do you think we're not? All we want is to be left alone. Can't you both understand? We'll call as soon as we get back. Bernice called Faye and gave her the report and said she thought it best to not call again.

Glenn and Faye finally solved the problem, they thought, by disconnecting the telephone. It didn't work. Faye was determined to get the last call, and being unable to get an answer, she called the desk clerk and had him check room 402 and call back and report if anything was wrong. He knew he shouldn't check anyone with a "Do not Disturb" sign on the door but being asked to do so, he checked anyway. This was the straw that broke the camel's back. Glenn answered the knock, not knowing what to expect. After the clerk gave him the message, Glenn became furious and told him to tell whoever called that they had just left for Alaska. The clerk said, "Are you sure you want me to tell them that?" Glenn replied, "Tell them what I told you. Thanks and good night." After the clerk left, everything turned out like most honeymoons do.

The next morning Glenn and Joy actually considered moving to Alaska. Could you blame them? Faye, Bernice, Lester, and Clyde felt washed out, guilty, and a little shaky, wondering if the couple might actually move to Alaska.

Maybe they woke up to the fact that when a couple marries it's time to let them live their own lives just like they had lived theirs. Most parents like to load their children down with advice, which is good if it's given in the right way. It's always best to give advice when there's no one around to hear it.

Do you agree? I do.

So long!

See ya!

COMPLAINING CHARLENE

From the first day Charlene was talking plainly, all she wanted to do was complain. She fussed if her mother put too much milk in her cereal or got her toast too brown, and Mom never seemed to fix her clothes like she wanted them. If the dress was too long and mom hemmed it for her, then she complained about it being too short. Her socks were always too big, and her shoes pinched her toes.

School days were unbearable. Charlene thought the teacher was partial to the other students, because she didn't call on her before she did the others, and, to hear her tell it, she always had to be last in the lunch line. She thought she had a prettier voice than anyone in school, but since she didn't, Carrie was usually called on to sing "America." Charlene could always be seen talking to all the other students about Carrie.

At home she had the same problem with her brothers and sisters. She constantly complained that her parents thought more of them than they did of her, and she pouted and pouted.

Charlene kept complaining as she grew up. She was now at the pimple age. She didn't have just one pimple, she had pimples by the dozens. She was very unhappy; she complained constantly because her brothers and sister and most of her friends didn't have pimples. She asked daily why she had pimples, saying it just wasn't fair: "Everything happens to me."

A few years later, Charlene was in her middle teens. Mom hoped she would grow out of her complaining, but the years just brought on more agony for family and Charlene's few friends. Some say it is in the genes, others say it's in the mind. Maybe it's for pity or maybe just attention. Whatever it was and wherever it came from, Charlene sure had plenty of it.

Charlene had been to the beauty shop, where she was never known to be satisfied with anything, especially a permanent. She raved and stormed about her hair. The last one she got the operator didn't put enough curl in it. Tonight was the high school football game, and Gloria would be there and her hair always looked better than Charlene's. Johnny (Charlene's boyfriend) liked to pass compliments on Gloris; he'd be sure to pay more attention to her than he would to Charlene, for Gloria always flirted with him.

Charlene was complaining about how much better Gloria's jeans fit than hers, and she blamed her mom for that, saying she didn't make her eat like she should, and she got fat where she didn't need to be. "I can't wear shorts because it's all mom's fault. She let me stand on my legs when I was a baby and it made my legs bow," Charlene said. She couldn't stop at that. She brought up having a long nose and said her mother read the story of Pinocchio over and over before she was born and had marked her by reading the story.

Charlene and Johnnie went to the ballgame, and to Charlene it was a disaster. She always pulled for her alma mater and this was the homecoming game, and her team lost. She said it was the referees' fault; they were partial to the other team. She complained and complained, turned blue in the face, and even started her temper ritual. Johnny threatened to leave, and for once, old Charlene calmed down and didn't complain anymore until they got up to leave. Then she found out that someone had spilled Coke on the seat, plus they had lost their big wad of chewing gum while yelling. Charlene had the misfortune of having wet pants plus the chewing gum right on the seat of her jeans. Poor Johnny heard about that all the way home and was so put out that he let her open her own car door and refused to kiss her goodnight, after she had already puckered up for a biggie. Poor Charlene complained all the rest of the night, or until the last one in the family covered their ears up to keep from hearing about it.

Morning came too soon, and poor Charlene awoke with a migraine headache, all because Johnnie had failed to kiss her. Maybe her face was strained from the puckering procedure that lasted so long and she was unable to unpucker it. I sure wouldn't ask her why she couldn't unpucker, for I detest hearing complaints, especially over faded love.

Charlene could be pretty when she wanted to be, but, as they say, "pretty is as pretty does." When she was asleep, she looked like a sleeping beauty; that is, to some people like poor Johnny.

No one knows how Charlene got a job in a local doctor's office as receptionist, but somehow she did. This gave her another chance to complain about being sick, saying the patients just wanted attention and they didn't even look sick. Some people thought that the job might break Charlene from her complaints, but she just learned more ways to complain.

Time went on and Johnnie couldn't have any luck dating other girls, so he proposed to Charlene. She jumped at the proposal but just couldn't keep from complaining because he hadn't proposed earlier.

Plans were in big fashion for the wedding. Everything was being carried out just like Charlene wanted it, except she worried about the weather. She was sure it would rain, and, being in November, the rain could turn to sleet or even snow, and if it snowed they couldn't take their honeymoon, and they would have to put it off until early spring, and she might be pregnant by then, and they would never get a honeymoon. After she wore that thought out, she came up with another one. If it should rain or snow, it might get her wedding gown wet, and the sequins might fall off. Or what if Johnny got his shoes and pants muddy? He was so careless; then he'd look just awful.

The day finally came for the wedding and Charlene was so happy she forgot to complain. Can you believe it? Well, she forgot for just a little while until they started making the pictures. Johnny forgot to smile in one of them, and Charlene noticed it and thought he might be sick, or maybe his wisdom tooth was hurting him again.

To make this truthful or untruthful story, whichever way you read it, short, they had a nice honeymoon trip, came back, and got settled down, with Charlene having more complaints than they had wedding gifts. The complaints lasted for one year, and guess what happened then–Johnnie and Charlene became the surprised parents of quadruplets, two sons and two daughters, and to this day Charlene hasn't complained once. Some say she is happy for once; while others say she doesn't have time to be happy. Keeping four bottles filled and washing all those diapers, there's just not much time to complain. Johnny told her if she started it again, he'd see that she might have four more babies to wash diapers for. That was warning enough to shut down Charlene's complaining.

So long!

See ya!

BESSIE

Bessie was a fair young lady, a very undignified person who spoke in a high pitched voice. She loved chewing gum and never slowed down in chewing it, and was known to be able to pop and crack it louder and longer than anyone had ever been known to do. Her biggest enemies were biscuits, gravy potatoes, cornbread, beans, milkshakes, ice cream, cake, pies, and large amounts of in-between snacks of chocolate candy that the old rich oil tycoon, Andy Grady, kept her well supplied with, trying his best to make a hit with her.

Bessie weighed a nice two hundred and seventeen and one half pounds to be exact, and she tried her best to be little and petite (except for the fact that she could not leave stuffing alone) and cramped herself into size 14 anytime she had plans. She was forced to push gassy food away from her plate, for one little belch would probably burst open the seams of her pretty ruffled dress. Mr. Grady was so much in love with Bessie, he could see no faults in anything she might do.

Bessie decided she wanted to be an opera singer. No one ever told her she could sing, but once Bessie made up her mind an army could not change her. She hinted the idea to the old tycoon, and he thought it was a wonderful idea and offered to bear the expense for lessons. Bessie began the lessons, but all she got out of it was a little experience.

Time elapsed and her voice teacher was forced to inform her that her voice was more appropriate for hog calling than it was for opera. The teacher made a mint out of Andy Grady before she would admit that opera singing was not meant for Bessie. So Bessie approached Mr. Grady with another idea, and, putting on an act of being heart-broken over not being able to sing opera, asked Mr. Grady to buy a farm and supply it with animals, especially with hogs. Mr. Grady thought, "If I buy a farm and all the animals Bessie mentioned, maybe she will marry me." It took some time, but he found a farm just like Bessie wanted. It had a house on it that anyone could be happy in, with fourteen rooms and six baths, all recently redecorated.

Mr. Grady proposed again. This proposal made the seventh time he had asked her, and by now Bessie was really wanting hold of his checkbook. She finally agreed to become Mrs. Grady, for although she had always been a big flirt, she had finally come to the conclusion that younger men were not interested in her. They were always giving her a cold shoulder; maybe that why she had arthritis in her shoulders. The feelings between the two who would soon marry were not mutual. Mr. Grady was marrying for love, and Bessie was marrying strictly for his bank account and was dreading giving up her freedom. But she liked the idea of living on a big farm in a beautiful house and having hogs to practice calling, which could lead to her being the winner of all hog calling in the U.S. of America, and, she thought she might even try out for the best in Canada and Russia.

Bessie started stroking Mr. Grady's hair and cuddling closer to him. Sweetly she asked if he would buy her a three-karat diamond ring, saying that when she would give her hog calling demonstration to big audiences, she would like to have the biggest diamond of all hog callers. Mr. Grady said, "Well, this year has been a whopper. I'm opening up lots of new oil wells and money is no problem with me, so why don't I buy you a five karat?" After hearing that statement Bessie moved over closer (much closer) to Mr. Grady and gave him an extended kiss. Fame and fortune were the two F's Bessie had always lived for and Mr. Grady had fortune, so maybe Bessie could use that to get fame.

Betsy got to work on her wedding plans, and everyone seemed to take a great interest in the oncoming marriage. Some of the churchgoing women finally persuaded Bessie to buy a size 42 wedding gown instead of a size 14 like the dresses she had been miserable in for the past number of years. This would certainly be the biggest wedding ever to be in Spruce Pines Church. Mr. Grady even had new carpet put in the sanctuary of the church, new lighting installed, and air conditioning put in, for he didn't want his sweet Bessie getting hot and having her much-too-much rouge running down her face. This was the busiest time of Bessie's life, as she made plans for the wedding and saw that her gown was sewn to perfection. With all the yards and yards of lace and diamond sequins to be sewn on it (some people thought they were real diamonds–they were even sewn on the train, which was twelve feet long), it took the seamstress two weeks to get the dress all ready.

The day of the wedding finally came and the florist had done an exceptionally good job with dozens and dozens of red and gold roses. Poor lovesick Mr. Grady wanted red roses for love, and Bessie wanted gold for what gold stands for, Since gold currency is locked up in Fort Knox, maybe Bessie should have had greenery. Anyway, the decorations were beautiful. Just as Bessie was about to start down the aisle, old lady Maltie Creekmore came in and stumbled over the train, which was so long it came out the door of the church, and almost fell. Maltie was too lazy to pick her feet up and too farsighted to see the train. Luckily she didn't get it dirty, for Maltie always played sick and had worn the new bedroom shoes her kids had given her for Christmas. They were green with Santa Claus designs all around them.

Mr. Grady was a little man only five feet and one inch tall, and his head had been bald long before he hit it rich in his oil fields. He had a little white mustache that he kept curled at the ends. They say love is blind, so that's good for Mr. Grady. He always looked up to Bessie for she was six feet and three and one half inches tall. It was easier looking up at her instead of around her.

The organist was playing "Here Comes the Bride" and Bessie marched down the aisle, looking on both sides to see who she could see. The wedding was carried out beautifully. She chose for the soloist to sing her favorite song, "Lonesome Valley." A few sniffs could be heard all over the church; either the music brought back memories of a departed loved one or people were allergic to roses. The wedding vows were long and touching and more sniffs were heard, but when the five-carat diamond was placed on Bessie's finger you could see envy in every woman there.

The caterers were fantastic. They were professionals and knew the tricks. They served a cake so large that it covered a big portion of a large table, plus everything they had ever served at weddings before. Bessie took the biggest piece of cake and took a whopping big bite. While she was still gasping for breath, she crammed a big bite in Mr. Grady's mouth, and he almost choked. Since Bessie wasn't lovesick, she ate and ate and then ate some more. Mr. Grady just picked at this and that while he made sure that his darling Bessie got all the food she wanted.

As they started to leave, the Rolls Royce came up and the chauffeur opened the door. Someone heard poor, starved Bessie say, "I can't wait to get to a restaurant where I can get all the seafood I can eat." Everybody else went home full of food and plenty of sympathy for Mr. Grady.

So long!

See ya!

EFFIE'S GREEN HAT

Effie had worn black hats for the last ten years, ever since the doctor told grandma she didn't have much longer to live. Grandma is now 87. Then there's Aunt Flo, who moved in with Grandma when her husband, Wilford, died eight years ago. Aunt Flo will not give permission for her age to be told. Looking at Aunt Flo and considering her being next in line to grandma, we all think she must be around 85.

Effie finally gave up on the deaths of either of the two and went shopping down at Wal-Mart. They had put out their new selection of summer hats, and there it was, right in front of Effie: a beautiful bright green hat. Effie snatched it off the mannequin, turned to a mirror, and put it on. She thought she looked snazzy in it, even if she hadn't washed her hair in two weeks and had been out picking strawberries all week. The price of the hat was reasonable, and Effie liked the pretty pink rose on the side of it. It did make old Effie look younger, and she was beginning to turn a new leaf. She was beginning to notice Fred glancing his eyes at pretty women, and that's one thing that Effie would not tolerate, having Fred looking twice at other women.

Effie paid for her hat at the check-out lane and went proudly out the door to the car where Fred was fidgeting, waiting on her. He liked the hat and promised to buy her a new dress the next time they came to Wal-Mart. Well, Effie went home with a light heart and pocket book, for she had paid for the hat with dimes, nickels, and some quarters.

Effie had made up her mind for no more pre-mourning for Grandma, and she had full intention to wear it to Grandma's funeral, that is, if she outlived her.

The next Saturday, Fred came in and told Effie he was going back to Wal-Mart for some bolts and screws. This time he didn't ask her to come along. She was so well pleased with the idea that all of a sudden, she told Fred that she had lost a little weight and believed she could wear a size 20. Fred was listening very carefully at what she had said, but as far as Effie believed, she didn't think he had heard a word of what she was saying. Fred combed his hair and even changed shirts, kissed Effie on the ear, and started off to Wal-Mart. The main thing Fred was after was the new dress he had promised Effie.

Clerks are never available when you want advice on something. Fred went through all the size 20 dresses and couldn't decide which one would look better on Effie–the yellow one trimmed in lace or the purple two-piece dress? He finally decided on the yellow one. He also got his bolts and screws and headed for home.

Effie met him at the car, for she was so anxious to see the dress she couldn't wait until he got in the house. She tried being nonchalant and asked Fred if he got the bolts and screws he had gone after. She spied a Wal-Mart bag much too big to put bolts and screws in. After Fred had given Effie a report on a break-in in Revco the night before, he slowly gave her the bag. When Effie saw that pretty yellow dress trimmed in lace and tucks, she became speechless (for a change). Finally, her brain cleared enough that she said, "Thank you" to Fred, and then she said it again, and again. Really it sounded like a broken record. Fred wanted her to try it on right then. When Effie came out, Fred whistled for the first time in thirty years. To other people she didn't look nearly so good as Fred thought. But if Fred liked her in her new yellow dress and green hat, it just wasn't other peoples' business. For Effie loved her Fred more than words can say or be put on paper.

Effie was so carried away with her new outfit, she decided she wanted a permanent. She made an appointment for Wednesday at 9:00 a.m. The poor beauty operator used a big portion of a bottle of shampoo trying to get the accumulated grease and grime out of Effie's hair. Operators have days like that, but when she was through, she felt very rewarded, for she had turned soured sweat into fluffy curls. After Effie was handed a mirror, she said, "I can't see myself, for that woman with all the pretty curls is standing in my way."

Joy, the operator, got so tickled she bit her tongue to keep from laughing, and she was beginning to think she would have to go to a doctor for stitches, but finally it quit bleeding and Effie recognized her own dress. She kept looking and admiring herself until it was time for lunch, and the beauticians persuaded her to go home. Joy had had all she could take for one day. She did take time to tell Effie her hair would stay pretty a long time if she kept it washed regularly.

What did Fred think about it? Well, you should have heard it, and actions speak louder than words. After all, they were in their own bedroom, and it's none of our business what took place.

Aunt Flo called Effie and told her that Grandma wasn't feeling well, and she should come over. Effie was thinking of Grandma's egg and butter money she had saved all through the years. She told Fred to rush her over there and wouldn't let Fred roll the window down, afraid it would ruin her hair in the wind. Effie got there just in time to see poor Grandma draw her last breath. Effie tried hard to put on a fake faint and failed. She tried screaming and that didn't work. She just decided that money talks, and she stayed calm and collected. That is, she was ready to collect as soon as Grandma was laid to rest.

The funeral turned out well. Grandma had lots of friends and relatives. Effie stood tall and straight at the head of the casket. Inwardly she wished she had a bottle of tears to put in her eyes to show grief.

Effie wore her yellow dress with lace and ribbon and the green hat with the pink rose on it. And, I forgot to tell you, she had bought a bottle of perfume at the Family Dollar Store for 75 cents. Maybe she had used too much, for you could smell it when you first entered the funeral home. Maybe that's why she couldn't faint; then again she might have thought that if she put on a fake faint she could fall and mash her pretty green hat. She had gotten over wearing black when she found out how pretty green and yellow looked on her, or that was what Fred thought. Many people think Fred is color blind.

Grandma was laid to rest beside Grandpa in a lonely cemetery, where only dead people stay. Effie forgot about trying to look pretty. She even forgot about her pretty outfit and did manage to shed a few tears.

Now poor Aunt Flo lives alone with only her memories of her late husband and how Grandma used to play the old pedal organ and sing "In the Sweet By and By." Maybe Effie will be able to cry when Aunt Flo dies, but who knows. You know life is uncertain, but death is sure.

So long!

See ya!

JULIA AND FURMAN

Julia and Furman were married in early spring in a simple wedding in the chapel of the Cedar Lake Presbyterian Church. Only the parents of the couple attended. Well, of course, the preacher was there, or they wouldn't have been lawfully married.

Julia was a very pretty bride, dressed simply in a short white dress and shoes, her black hair short and wavy, and shining beautifully. Just a year or so ago she was runner-up for Miss South Carolina. They had a double ring ceremony and made the promise, "until death do us part." You know, at many weddings that promise doesn't last until all the wedding cake is digested. Furman was a well-built, muscular man, having the potential to be a football player, in addition to being handsome.

Good jobs weren't plentiful in the small town of Friendsville. Furman was a supervisor in a cotton mill, where he made a reasonable amount of money to support his new bride. Because of his insistence on being the "breadwinner," Julia gave up her job in a local hospital and became the proverbial housewife. Furman had always dreamed of being a good provider, and since Julia was careful with money, they led good normal lives. At times they were even able to take short vacations.

Days passed into months and the months into years, until 25 of them had flown by. They wondered, just like we do, where the years had gone. In those 25 years they had been blessed with two sons and two daughters, and with careful planning they had put them through college, with degrees form Presbyterian College in Clinton, South Carolina. It had been penny pinching and nervewracking, but they had done it. Accomplishment well done, I'd say.

Julia's willingness to cooperate with Furman's determination to be the bread-winner forced Julia to use her talents to sew for her daughters and to break fingernails off digging in the garden to grow vegetables to freeze and can. Taking time for all this work left very little time to keep up the once good looks she had when Furman married her. (Poor Julia—that's what happens though.) Her pretty black shiny hair had turned to silver around her temples, and even her smile was dropping, when she felt like smiling! Things just weren't like they used to be, which happens to people sometimes, especially when you become fiftyish. There were wrinkles forming around her eyes and upper lip–you know the little streaks you get dirt in and you have to scrub to get it out. That's true–just ask anyone over fifty or even seventy and they'll agree. The wrinkles were formed mainly from worry over her four children, listening for foot steps returning home from 12:00 A.M. until the wee hours of morning. Now that will cause wrinkles by the dozen.

Furman had taken a new look on life now that the children had all flown the coop and he and Julia were left alone. You know at 55 some men try to show the public they are still young; some try to even look handsome, wearing dentures, toupees, and a sexy smile, making eyes at young women. You know what! That's exactly what happened to old Furman. He was failing to see what he had once seen in Julia. Of course she had put on some extra pounds, mostly around her waist. (Like I have done in my 70's.) She sure wouldn't be eligible to enter a Mrs. South Carolina beauty contest. But she was the same loyal wife he had married years ago, he just took her for granted, not knowing or even thinking that sometimes the tide will turn.

Gossipers were busy asking each other, "Have you heard about Furman and that young woman who has moved into the apartment across the street from Jane Bush's apartment? Jane says she sees Furman Fuller go in her apartment regularly. I wish someone would tell Julia, but being the good Christian I am I don't want people to get the impression of me being a gossiper." Once Freeda told Pricilla if she wanted Julia to know about it, to tell her herself. That took the wind out of pious Pricilla, but the episode continued and poor Pricilla couldn't keep quiet any longer: she told herself it was all right to tattle, so she called Callie and told her about it, and that 's all it took. Julia heard before the sun went down. Julia had not been in the dark. She was seeing for herself and waiting for the proper time. Much like a cat catching a mouse, you have to be patient and quiet.

A letter came to Julia from her high school class president telling her when their 30-year class reunion would be. Now was Julia's time to retaliate. The reunion would be in a short time–time to get things her way for once in 25 years. Since she had more time now to think of herself, she started taking exercise daily and staying off fatty foods. In a short time she could see her weight falling off. She kept the reunion to herself, thinking what is salt for the goose is salt for the gander.

One day Julia asked Furman for the car, because she wanted to go in to town for a few things. Furman gave her a questioning look and said, "Okay." He was scared she might be hearing things he'd rather she didn't hear.

Julia first made an appointment with a very popular hairdresser for a permanent, which she hadn't had in years. After that she went to an expensive dress shop and bought the prettiest and most expensive dress there, plus a girdle that pinched but took away the flab. (Who wouldn't wear one that pinched if it made you look girlish? I would.) Then she was off to a shoe store for the most fashionable shoes she could buy. She needed make-up, perfume, hand cream, nail polish. Then she asked herself, 'Where have I been through the years? Maybe Furman had a reason for stepping out on me, but he won't have it for long, for society here I come!" She went home feeling more like herself than she had felt in years, or much more than she had been feeling since Furman started his little fling.

Furman was sitting on the front porch steps, having an intuition that something was brewing and it wasn't coffee. As she started gathering up packages from the car, he knew it had happened. He noticed that she had lost weight and was walking with a rhythm in her step. She was singing a song they used to sing when they were dating. Furman looked with amazement as Julia came up. He said, "Looks like something has happened." Julia only smiled and said, "It has, and it will again."

Getting a little suspicious Furman stood up, stuttered a little trying to ask the right question but scared she might have heard too much and quite anxious for an answer. "Oh," replied Julia in a very flippant way, "I just thought I'd try getting my youth back again." Furman tried to assure her he liked her the way she was. Julia answered in a very icy tone, "I'm tired of being like I am, since you have made such a sudden change from an adult to a pre-teen." That statement really sunk in on old Furman. He realized his goose was cooked and not in honey but in sour grapes.

"I decided my motherly looks were over," said Julia. "Tomorrow I get a permanent for the first time in twenty years, and come inside, I'll show you my new outfit I got to wear to my 30-year class reunion." If Julia had had a feather, she sure could have floored him with it. While she was at it, she told old Furman if he could stay away from apartment B room 206 long enough, she would be delighted to have him go with her to the class reunion. "But if you can't," she said, "there will be a number of old friends that will be pleased to get to dance with me again. For instance, there is Bill, whom I used to date; he's a widower now. Then there's George and Pete, whom I've heard are divorced and looking for romance. Of course now Furman, if you decide to go, you've out grown your old suit, so you'll need a new one."

Furman had no intention for staying home while Julia went to the reunion. After tossing and turning, unable to sleep all night, Furman rolled out early and headed for town. He bought an expensive suit with accessories to match and didn't dare go by apartment B room 206.

When Julia and Furman had dressed in their new outfits, they saw something in each other they hadn't seen in years. Julia was as pretty as she was when she was nominated for Miss South Carolina and Furman didn't look so bad himself, even if he had put on weight around his waist.

The reunion turned out beautifully; everyone was happy to see each other again. As Julia and Furman bade each one good-bye and started for home, Furman decided it was the appropriate time to confess to his seeing the girl in apartment B. Julia said, "Well maybe throughout the years I have taken you for granted." They both agreed it was a lesson well learned. The sparkle in their eyes had been relit and they lived life again as it should be.

So long!

See ya!

CORA'S FIRST TRAIN RIDE

Well, there are lots of folks in Friendsville and in the county that have never traveled any more than to the county seat. You know, when you have to pay your taxes, get your car or marriage lisence, or get a form of some kind filled out. This story is about Cora, a lady who got a chance to travel, really travel. Most of us were jealous. At least, for a while.

Cora and N.T. were walking hand in hand out in the pasture field one bright sunny spring day. The wild flowers were bursting out in full bloom, and it somehow made expectations of love and marriage blossom in their minds. N .T. was kinda on the bashful order and was wanting to ask a very important question. Cora sensed the blundering question, and, looking up into N.T.'s face with an inquiring gesture, asked, "What are you going to say? Come on and say it." N.T. swallowed, cleared up his throat, had a bad coughing spell, turned red in the face, sneezed four times, stumbled and almost fell, and finally, after Cora rubbed the perspiration off his forehead and put a little kiss on the end of his nose, he finally popped the question. "Cora you are beautiful, adorable, and something about you makes my heart thump like thunder; actually, I could almost die." Swallowing, he repeated himself again, "Cora . . . Cora will you marry me?"

Cora tried to act surprised, and said, "I can't marry you now."

"Why?" exclaimed N.T. "Why won't you marry me? Don't you love me?"

"Oh yes," said Cora, "I love you dearly, but I must do one thing before I settle down. All my life I have wanted to ride a train, and I must do it before we get married."

N.T. studied over the situation. He wanted so much to have Cora as his own that he promised her he would take her on that much wanted train ride. "When can we go?" asked Cora. "Well," N.T. said, "I have only enough money saved to buy you two rings, a cook stove, cupboard, table, some chairs, a bed and dresser, and me a new suit, that is if I can sell my tobacco for a good price this fall to buy the suit. I promise, so help me. We'll ride the train someday just you wait and see." Cora couldn't turn down a chance of marriage to a good-looking guy like N.T.

N.T.'s name was Nathan Taylor, but everybody called him N.T. for short. Just thought I'd put that in so you know what his full name was.

They were married in a short time after the proposal. It wasn't a very extravagant wedding at all, but the knot was tied and Cora was now Mrs. Nathan Taylor Hodge, ready to be a responsible, understanding, loving housewife.

In two years little Maggie was born. She was a beautiful blue-eyed baby who looked like her mama, but she had N.T.'s dark curly hair and that added on to her beauty. There was another mouth to feed, and times were hard in 1910. Just no time or money to spend on a train trip, but Cora never gave up wishing.

Oops! Guess what happened two years later–little Maggie had a little brother and sister, which Grandma Hodge just had to name Pearle and Pulliam: since they were such beautiful names, that's what went down in the family Bible. The expense in bringing them up doubled and made it hard to make ends meet.

They loved the children dearly, and as time passed and the children grew, Cora sort of forgot about her promised train ride, except when she would hear the lonesome whistle and could see the train at a distance as it sped through the field looking like a black snake scaling around the curvy tracks.

One day several years later, N.T. came home from work, whistling and singing with joy. He had hit it lucky, which I won't take time to explain. I will say this: N.T. did not gamble, nor did he steal, and I'll also add he was very honest. He rushed into the house and, catching Cora unaware in his arms, he told her of getting some back pay. Was Cora dreaming, or was it real? Yes, it was real, and Cora and N.T. were going to Savannah, Georgia, on the train to see Aunt Lucy. They started making plans immediately.

Cora was so excited over the ending of her long wait for a train ride that she could scarcely believe tomorrow was the day for the reality. She had everything prepared. She and N.T. had their baths, separately of course, taken in the big number-10-size wash tub. Everything was in order for tomorrow. The one thing Cora couldn't control was that she just couldn't go to sleep. She counted four hundred and seventeen sheep and was just ready to pass into dreamland when suddenly two rams butted heads just as they were fixing to jump the rail fence, and tore it down. Poor Cora forgot how many she had counted and had to start all over again. Getting disgusted with the whole thing, she decided she'd just repeat the Pledge of Allegiance, but she got halfway through and forgot the rest.

Then something else ran through her mind: if George Washington's teeth were made of wood, she wondered if he ever got splinters off them when he'd eat beef jerky or a hard corn pone. It came to her very plainly that maybe he didn't have to eat beef jerky or hard corn pone, being President of the United States. Something else came to mind: what if the teeth started sprouting leaves? Wouldn't he have looked funny with leafy teeth? Again she was almost asleep, but N.T. started his loud snoring. Poor Cora was so exhausted she could take no more. She rolled out of bed and went to the guest bedroom, yanked the covers back and, in a frenzy, crawled in, and finally fell asleep.

When the roosters started crowing in the wee hours of morning, Cora was so fagged out she didn't hear them. Well, roosters are not like alarm clocks–they alarm more then once. N.T. never bothered to listen for them, and luckily for Cora the second crowing an hour later awakened her. Cora yelled for N.T. to get up, "This is the big day you promised me 20 years ago!" N.T. rolled out of bed rubbing his eyes and twisting a curl in his hair that never wanted to stay in place and finally got awake enough to eat the big breakfast Cora had prepared. She thought they should eat a full meal so they wouldn't get too hungry on the train. She had ham, gravy, grits, eggs, hot biscuits, molasses, honey, and fresh butter. It was good and they enjoyed it. Cora took time to clean the dishes, for they would be gone for five days and four nights. That was assuming Aunt Lucy was feeling well enough to entertain them.

Cora had their clothes all laid out to wear. She took off the flannel gown she had cooked breakfast in, and after putting on her corset and lacing it up, next came her eyelet embroidered petticoats. She then stopped to curl her hair with crimped metal curlers she heated in the lamp. Now she put on rouge and lipstick she had bought just for the trip. She was ready for her pretty navy satin dress with the crocheted collar she had made to wear with it. Next she put on the grey spool heeled slippers and got her blue velvet hat with a grey plume all around it. "Gosh," said N.T., "You are more beautiful than ever. You look as young as you did the day I proposed to you." Grabbing her, he kissed her and messed her hair, but she didn't mind, for she was happy and still in love with N.T. She said, "Just wait until I get my new grey coat on." N.T. looked flabbergasted; she hadn't bothered to tell him about the coat, but N.T. knew she needed it and just kept quiet. After all, she was just too pretty for him to complain.

N.T. was a tall slender man with black wavy hair and deep blue eyes. He was as handsome as Cora was attractive. He had spent much time polishing his shoes and dusting the derby he wore only on special occasions. Cora had taken great pains in pressing his special blue serge suit, and spent hours ironing his Sunday shirt starched in heavy homemade starch, plus the separate collar that was even stiffer than the shirt. Cora helped get his tie to look just right, too.

Cora checked again to see if N.T. had his pocketbook, for Glenn (their neighbor) would be there soon in his model T Ford to take them to the depot to catch the Southern train that would take them to Aunt Lucy and Uncle Floyds in Savannah Georgia. After waiting for endless minutes, they heard the rattle of the old model T coming down the road. N.T. grabbed the suitcase and, taking Cora's arm, marched down to the two-seater car. Glenn tried hard to be polite and rushed around the car to open the door, and just as he did, the car started rolling down the hill. He almost broke his neck racing after it. After catching up and seating himself, he slammed on the brakes in the middle of a big mud puddle and splashed muddy water all over the car. It was good N.T. and Cora were still several feet from the car, or they would have been dotted all over in mud and water.

Things usually turn out all right. They turned out alright this time, too. Being careful not to step in the mud, Cora and N.T. were soon in the car and on their way enjoying seeing the big coal-burning monster come huffing and puffing down the tracks with big clouds of smoke rolling out from the engine. Roaring at its loudest, the loud-sounding whistle that Cora loved to hear made chills run up Cora's back as the engine came to a halt; sparks of fire flew from the wheels, which caused Cora to almost collapse. As the door of the train opened, the conductor stepped out and checked their tickets, remarking, "Oh, you folks going all the way to Savannah, Georgia."

Cora hoped everyone was listening, but no one seemed to notice. After being helped up the steps in the train Cora and N.T. chose a seat by the window. In a few minutes the conductor called out, "All aboard! All aboard!" The door was closed and the old coal burner started huffing and puffing down the track. To Cora it seemed they were traveling the same rate of speed a jet would go today. It's mostly in one's mind, anyway. Hours passed and several passengers (who had ridden trains before) had fallen asleep, but not Cora and N.T., for every time N.T. would nod, Cora would see something exciting and wake him up. Cora didn't dare close her eyes, and every time she saw someone watching the train go by, she hoped they saw her and N.T. and, with wistful thinking, hoped they saw her pretty grey buttoned slippers. People on the train could see them and that helped keep up her ego, for she was real proud of N.T. in his nice pressed blue serge suit and black derby hat and nicely shined shoes. She still thought she was dreaming–and not counting sheep either. Time passes so quickly when you are enjoying something so fabulous as an unbelievable train ride.

Cora noticed the train was coming to a quick stop and hoped no cattle or horses were on the track. She had heard of that happening before, but this was much more exciting than having a horse or cow on the track.

A young man was standing in the middle of the track waving a red bandanna. The engineer called out, "Why did you stop my train? I have a schedule to make."

"But Mister," replied the young man, "Right around this curve is a big boulder that has fallen right on the track." Poor Cora and N.T. became very upset, not knowing if they could continue their long-planned trip to Savannah. Questions ran through their minds: What if they had to spend all their money on food while they waited, maybe for days. They had been told food was very expensive on the train. If that happened then they would have no money to buy gifts for Maggie, Pearle, and Pulliam (their three children). Then there were gifts for Aunt Bernice, Uncle Fred, N.T.'s parents, Cora's parents, the preacher, Glen, for he was so nice to bring them to the depot, and Cora's brother Ed who was keeping their children and making sure Maggie, who was 18, didn't court the elementary school teacher too much while they were gone. There was Pearle and Pulliam for Ed to look after, sixteen years old but not usually called sweet sixteen. Uncle Ed had to force them each morning to get up, eat breakfast, which wasn't up to their mama's, feed the cats and dogs, and dress for school. Taking advantage of their uncle, they were always late for school, and poor uncle Ed, had he been a woman, it would have taken a full bottle of Cardui to calm his nerves down.

Without going into details, the big boulder was soon removed and the young man was offered a lifetime pass on the railroad to go wherever he wished to go, but he just thanked them and walked away. Who knows, he could have been an angel. Again the train started its huffing and puffing and everyone became calm again, and that was another page for Cora to add to the memos she was keeping in her 5-cent tablet she had carefully brought along in her pocketbook. Looking out the window with her left eye to see what she could see, she was using her right eye to write it down. A bit complicated but she did it, for she wanted a lifetime memento of her precious, long-hoped for train ride to see Aunt Lucy and Uncle Floyd Carson.

The train slowed down and the conductor called out, "Next stop Savannah!" After the train stopped completely, N.T. and Cora knew the ride was over for the time being. Everyone got their baggage and started off the train. N.T. and Cora started looking for Aunt Lucy and Uncle Floyd, but the depot was crowded. They hadn't seen Aunt Lucy in several years. It turned out there had been a big change in her: she had put on a huge amount of weight, and her bright yellow hair had turned to silver. She wasn't any prettier now than she was when she was sweet sixteen. Maybe I'd better just say sixteen, for she was never very sweet.

Finally Lucy recognized Cora, and after much hugging and kissing and shrill giggles from Lucy, and deciding everyone had seen her, she and Uncle Floyd (Lucy's unattractive husband) directed them to the new 1920 Ford car they had just purchased after hearing N.T. and Cora were coming. They wanted to make a big impression on N.T., this being his first visit to the Lucy and Floyd Carson home. Lucy rushed around and soon had a bountiful supper prepared. She was careful to use her best white table cloth and fringed napkins and her blue willow china. N.T. and Cora were exhausted from their long train ride, and their stomachs were growling for food, and the food went down like snow falling in August–that is, after Uncle Floyd ended the lengthy prayer he had been practicing on for several days. They kept insisting on their guests eating more, and when the dessert was served Cora and N.T. could barely find room for a big piece of yellow cake covered with chocolate icing, and a bowl of Alberta peaches right out of a jar that Lucy had canned earlier. Aunt Lucy loved compliments on her food and started fishing for them. After Cora and N.T. expressed their compliments many times and convinced Lucy that the food was the best they had ever eaten and satisfying Aunt Lucy, Lucy and Floyd took their guests into the parlor where Floyd had a roaring fire in the fireplace and had their Aladdin lamp lit. Floyd got out his pipe and filled it with strong smelling burley he had gathered from his own tobacco patch.

After sitting down on the beautiful green velvet sofa, their supper began to digest. Aunt Lucy wanted N.T. to hear her heartwarming music on the organ. Lucy was three times too large for the organ stool, but she was able to keep her balance as she bore down on the pedals and keys. Floyd didn't want her to get all the compliments, so he laid his pipe on the mantle and cleared up his throat. His voice was as strong as a lion's, and Lucy's voice resembled a screaming hyenna. They wanted to provide entertainment, and they did, such as it was. They chose their favorites: Nellie Gray, Swing Low Sweet Chariot, Clementine, Red Wings, Maple on the Hill, and She'll be Comin Around the Mountain, which was getting popular at the time. It became boring before they decided to stop for the night. Much to the dissatisfaction of N.T. and Cora, here came Lucy with a big pan of roasted peanuts, and Floyd, not to be outdone, followed her with a big platter of delicious popcorn balls. He had been told by a number of hungry people that he could make better popcorn balls than anyone. Poor Cora and N.T. were forced to indulge.

Finally Lucy prepared the bed in the guest bedroom. On the pillows were her favorite pillowcases, which she had embroidered and decorated with crocheted lace. It was obvious to Cora that Lucy had spent hours ironing the starched sheets on the bed. Lucy put her four prized quilts on mostly for show, for the room wasn't that cold, and she told Cora how long it took her to piece and quilt them. Poor Cora and N.T. were so tired and full of food they could have slept on concrete, but the bed was much better than that. On top of the straw mattress was a goose-feather tick, and without a lullaby, Cora and N.T. fell asleep. If the roosters crowed in Savannah they sure didn't hear them.

Sleeping much later than they were used to sleeping at home, a knock on the door aroused them. It was Aunt Lucy calling them to breakfast. To Cora and N.T. this was like being in paradise. The southern hospitality was more than they could comprehend. Cora even asked herself if she were dreaming.

Floyd and Lucy tried to show them everything they could of the old historic town. They boasted about Eli Whitney inventing the cotton gin near Savannah in 1793, and helping to make cotton the South's most important crop. They saw all the well-kept houses built near the sidewalks many years ago. It was just more than Cora could imagine being real, but she kept it all down on paper so that she could relive it many times in the years to come.

The days flew by, and it was soon time to leave this beautiful old city and go back to country life.

After buying gifts for their family and friends, Cora and N.T. talked it over and thought it would be more than right that they buy the host and hostess gifts, since they had been so gracious to them and had shown them such a lovely time.

For Floyd's gift, N.T. chose a new Kaywoodie pipe, since his old one was strong enough to walk. It was a fancy one and Floyd was well pleased with it. Cora thought Aunt Lucy would love to be among the first in Savannah to wear make-up, so she bought her a box of rouge and bright red lipstick. Lucy was so well pleased with the purchase she couldn't wait to get a mirror. She just smeared it on without looking, and to tell the truth, it really looked messy, but Lucy was delighted.

The train pulled up to a stop and after many thanks and expressions of gratitude plus goodbye hugs and kisses and invitations to "please come back soon," Cora and N.T. boarded the train. As it pulled out and they saw the last glimpse of Aunt Lucy and Uncle Floyd, Cora said to N.T., "You know what, I'm glad we waited all these years to make this trip." N.T. said, "You know, I am too. If we had taken it earlier it would all be over, and Savannah wouldn't have been nearly so big."

So long!

See ya!

GRANDPA SHERMAN AND THE GHOSTS

It was the annual get-together for the Murray family. Sherman and Sally had been married for 43 years and were the proud parents of seven children. Each year at this particular time in August, it was traditional to have all seven children and their spouses, their twenty grand-children and their spouses, plus six great-grandchildren all come home for a hallelujah get-together.

Sherman and Sally worked from one get-together to the next, picking up pieces from the last one and making plans on how to improve the next one. Much planning and discussion were needed. Sally knew the likes and dislikes of each person, and there seemed to be more dislikes than likes. The spouses were from all over, two from Cuba, one from the French-speaking province of Canada, and two were Mexicans.

The problem of keeping peace among them and feeding and bedding them all sometimes ran into more than poor Sally could take, but the garden had turned out real well. Sherman had great success in getting rid of the pesky rabbits that usually got their share of the Murray garden. Sally had shed gallons of sweat saving everything that ripened. This get-together was the one big thing of the year.

Their big three-story house was opened up and aired out and linens were freshly washed and put on the beds. Even the one bed in the west wing of the house on the third floor had been changed, though Sherman always saw to cleaning that room himself. He spoke of ghosts being in that particular room, how they swished by the bed and made moaning, groaning noises and even music that could be heard at a distance. Sally was happy to give Sherman the job, as she was busy rolling out the rollaway beds that had been stored in the attic since last year.

Poor Sally was so tired and nervous she was forced to take a nerve pill so she could be rational when the guests arrived. Sherman had already seen to his part of it while cleaning up the ghost room, and he followed his work with a dose of garlic which he claimed was food for arthritis. He thought it took care of the smell of the "white lightening" he had just got through indulging in.

Everything was in order now, even the bouquets Sally had just freshly made. Sherman had his new sneakers on and a fresh T-shirt, Sally had on for the first time the Christmas dress that their grandson James and wife Feleste had given her, even though it was August. I forgot to mention that James had married Feleste, a Bostonian, and she couldn't or wouldn't try to get used to Southern hospitality. But to balance them out, there was Clyde, married to a girl from the British Isles. Sally liked her very much, for she called Sally Grandmother Sally and was the reason Sally went out and bought two boxes of mascara and always used more than was necessary.

Sally had every big pot and pan on the large kitchen range loaded with all the vegetables and meat that could be mentioned, cooked and ready to serve. The long dining table with all the extra leaves had been set and covered over for days. Cups and glasses had even been taken out of the shelves and washed.

Suddenly Sherman saw a van turn the curve in the road at Leonard Carlisle's place. "Look!" Sally shouted, "Sherman, that looks like Sherman Jr.'s van," and suddenly they heard the horn start blowing. Sherman and Sally rushed out to the fence railing to await their arrival. The doors opened, and ten relatives rolled out. Hugging and kissing took place, and exchanges of 'how the kids are growing' and 'so glad Sherman III and Marvin could come.' These were Sherman's sons, just too backward to ask for dates, and, not being very handsome themselves, the girls didn't ask them.

Now they had all heard thorough the years about the haunted room and Sherman Jr.'s family always made it a point to get there first and get the bedroom on the second floor facing north, for they didn't want the ghost room and also didn't want to have the sun shine in on them and wake them early in the morning before the ham and biscuits were done.

Sherman always made it a point to tell the ghost stories to each carload of relatives. He changed it from year to year. He spoke of how he liked to go to the ghost room when things got a little hectic with him and Sally, and how he related to the ghosts. Poor Sally would get in such a frenzy when he told these stories she would have to put hair spray on her hair to help hold it down.

The story was that Sherman had viewed the house well before buying it, and in one small bedroom was a crack in the wall. After investigating, he found it wasn't a crack at all: it was a sliding door into a small compartment, just right for hiding Sherman's "white lightening" secretly from Sally. When Sally didn't get her way, she sometimes put on unreasonable acts, such as rolling her eyes back in her head, trembling, and making moaning noises just like Sherman said that ghosts made. I guess that's where he got the idea. Anyway, she pretended to be grieving over the step-mother that she detested who had passed on 14 years ago. Sherman would then give in to whatever Sally was asking and take off to the haunted room to meditate or take a snort of his white lightening.

More guests arrived in more cars, vans, motorcycles, pickups, and trailers to fill up the parking space at the Murray residence. Everyone arrived casual except Feleste, who acted her Bostonian upbringing, even to wearing flimsy nighties in which she loved to expose her well-built body, which made all the mothers a bit jealous as they were trying to satisfy their squally offspring. It was well known that the Murray family had the worse spoiled kids of anyone registered in the United States and maybe Australia.

After everyone had hugged and kissed, and ooed and aahed, and expressed their feelings of how well everyone was holding their own, Sherman rang the dinner bell as he did when the children were all growing up. Then Sally asked Sherman to return thanks even though his breath did smell of white lightening tapered off with garlic. The tables were covered with Sally's beautiful self-embroidered table cloths, which were sure to be splashed with tea and food–roast beef, lamb chops, fried chicken with gravy, green beans, potato salad, two congealed salads, slaw, fried okra, peas with carrots, one gallon of fresh apples, collard greens, banana pudding, two pound cakes, six chocolate pies, five gallons of tea, and a 50-cup coffee maker (they had borrowed from the church) full of coffee. Rosalee, Clarence's daughter by his ex-wife (who came every year because she loved all the relatives) didn't like anything poor Grandma had prepared and asked to be taken out to Hardees for a roast beef sandwich.

Somehow everyone was busy stuffing their own starved stomachs and failed to notice poor spoiled Rosalee and to see that she had lost out in going to Hardees and had eaten until she had to have Gas-X before everyone was through eating. Clarence's ex-wife was too busy eating to hear Rosalee wish for Hardee's roast beef, or she would have insisted on Clarence taking her, mostly for an excuse to go along, for she was still deeply in love with the two-timer.

After everyone ate until their eyes bulged out, the men slid out to the spacious living room, while the women all turned in to clean up the dishes. Even Feleste carried dishes to the kitchen, being very careful not to get anything on her Chinese silk dress.

After a while the dishes were all cleaned away, and food was prepared for breakfast. All the women headed for the living room. It was really good to have everyone there, even to Iva Lee the ex-wife. Sally was trying to be calm, for she really enjoyed having her family all home. Everyone was talking, trying to keep Sherman from getting on the haunted room tales, which he changed quite often, causing some of the in-laws to sort of doubt. The kids were sleepy and fussy and one by one their mothers tucked them in bed. After the kids were put away for the night, everyone relaxed and started more or less bragging of their experiences and well doings of the past year.

There was Carleen who had won the beauty contest at the community college. Garland was a top-notch ball player and had also won many trophies ice skating. Marie won the prize at the county fair for making the best cherry preserves. Opal won the blue ribbon for the prettiest crocheted centerpiece.

Don sat petrified; he was scared his wife Arlene might tell why they had to borrow money to make the trip. He didn't want anyone to know that the law caught him just a tenth of a mile from the state line, where Don had just a little too much under his belt from the same thing Grandpa Sherman liked.

Arlene looked at Don, and he looked so scared that Arlene thought it would be shameful for all the other good church-going people to put her Don down in religious estimation. It wasn't only Don; some more of the family had the same habit Grandpa Sherman had: there was Curtis, David, Faye, George, Otto Jr., Clarence Jr., and weakly little Jared, who always played sickly.

Everyone enjoyed visiting and eating home made ice cream, pop corn and roasted peanuts, before slipping off to bed. Each one avoided the west wing bedroom to the right. Don and Arlene took the one to the left and they were so worn out after driving three hundred miles, they wouldn't have cared to be carried away with a ghost. But nothing happened and they drifted off into sleepy town very soon.

At last Sherman and Sally were cozy in their own bed with their favorite night shirts on, and even though Sally was worn to a frazzle, she fell asleep knowing all her offspring were safe and happy. She couldn't be sure about Feleste, but she was from Boston.

Sally was so worn out she slept until 7 o'clock. She called Sherman and insisted he get up and help with breakfast. He didn't like the idea too well and decided to get help. One by one a sleepy-eyed woman would get up and offer help that Sally had a job for. Iva Lee volunteered to make biscuits, because Clarence used to brag on them being good when he still belonged to her.

She made them and they turned out good, and Clarence flashed his eyes up at her every time he got one, which included six in all. Some of the women fried eggs, some made pancakes, and one was in charge of the sausage frying. Sally cooked the grits, And even the little six-year-old granddaughter Ellen poured the cereal out, spilling part of it on the floor.

Again a good meal was enjoyed, not leaving much of anything for the dogs and cat. Clarence even swiped the gravy bowls out clean with the last biscuit, mostly because Iva Lee had made them.

Sally surprised the whole family by saying, "It's time to get ready for church." Excuses started springing up from all of them. Some had sore throats, one had bursitis, Clarence had a headache, which caused Iva Lee to come down with an earache so she would be left with Clarence.

Sally ignored everything; she would not take no for an answer. She wanted her family all in church one more time, mostly for the Reverend to see. After being convinced they couldn't win out, everyone started dressing with what they had brought along. It so happened Feleste had brought church-going clothes for herself and Larry (Larry is Curtis' youngest son, quite up to par). Sally was rushing everyone, persuading the men to wear ties, even if they did wear sport shirts and sneakers. She started bringing out ties the kids had given Sherman for the last twenty years. It served them right for they could have given him something different occasionally. The women just had to wear hose whether they wanted to or not. Sally started looking through drawers collecting hose that had been given to her, even some with seams in the back.

Finally everyone was dressed, but only Feleste and Larry's outfits could be called appropriate. Sally gave strict orders to all sit on pews together, which filled one third of the church. Even though Sally missed singing in the choir, she felt richly blessed having all her family present, and, being able to sing louder than anyone in the church, she knew
she would be heard by all present.

When the Reverend asked for the visitors to please stand, all the Murrays stood up. He became so frightened that he forgot what he was going to preach on, and he started out on whiskey drinking and women being untrue to their husbands.

He preached and preached, getting louder and louder, scaring the poor children into hysterics and tramping on the toes of most everybody in the church.

He was so hysterical himself that he had forgotten about the little sin he and Sally had committed which he almost lost has wife over and, had she squealed, his Reverend title. Anyway he continued preaching, repeating the same thing over and over. Finally, Sherman could take it no longer and he took a step forward. Shortly a son went up, then another one, the daughters-in-law, grandsons–everyone but Feleste and Larry. It just wasn't Feleste's style, for she was a Bostonian and she was fast making one out of Larry. All confessions were made, handshaking ended, and the Reverend had the benediction way past the usual closing time. The Murrays rushed home feeling light-hearted and hungry. Lunch was rushed up, for it was high time the family was on their way.

Sherman called the family in the living room and told them he would openly make another confession if they'd promise to never tell the Reverend. They all promised. Then he told them how he had fooled them all these years about the haunted room. "Well, I'll confess," he said, "I was the ghost, it was my place of seclusion, a place where I could have my little drink of white lighting and not bother Sally for she didn't like the idea at all. The crack in the wall behind the chifferobe is a swinging door that leads to my little hideout where I have kept my white lighting all these years. Now the ghost is gone and my conscience is clear. Who else has a confession to make?"

Slowly, one by one, they made their confessions. It was Sally's turn, and she blushingly told of her fling with the Reverend and how his wife had caught them and threatened to tell the whole congregation about it if she ever caught them again. The men looked around at their wives to see if they had any confessions to make, but they were all gone. They were all seen down at the pond throwing pebbles in the water to make little ripples. Everyone was buried in their own thoughts. Finally they returned to the house, and as far as the family knows, the women were all free of guilt. Even Feleste threw pebbles in the pond. Guess she's O.K. too.

Everybody packed their vehicles, kissed each other good-bye, and the family found out after all this time why Clarence and Iva Lee had separated: just too much white lighting. Maybe they'll get back together now that Clarence has confessed. We ought to know by next year when they have the family reunion.

Finally the last car went around the curve where Sherman and Sally had watched them come in just yesterday. Sally said to Sherman, "You know I dread going back in the house; it sure will be lonesome. But I'll say next year, they'll all be wanting to sleep in the west wing bedroom." Sherman agreed, and they started back in the house holding hands.

Guess it was hard having to go back to an empty house again.

So long!

See ya!

POOR SICK CLAUDIA

Claudia loved telling people how sick she was. It wasn't only Claudia and her doctor who knew the results of her permanent sickness. Her friends and associates had learned long ago to never approach her with any information of anyone's sickness. If it happened to slip out, you were in for an hour or so of her identical case of the same thing, always much worse than what Jane or John had. When insurance companies were at the peak of paying hospital bills, poor Claudia took advantage of it like millions of people did. She spent 150 days in the hospital the first year of her medical insurance payoff.

She first complained of dizziness, which at the time, the doctor (who was a fee-grabbing physician whose name I won't mention since he was a big supporter of mine when I ran for County Executive; however I lost the race) told her she needed hospitalization care. He told her to enter the hospital immediately for tests and bed rest. Claudia did take time to get a new permanent and go shopping for new pajamas, matching house shoes, and robe, knowing she would be spending all the time the doctor and hospital personnel would allow.

After entering the hospital, her dizziness didn't immediately leave. Many blood tests, EKG's, and brain scans were given, and they even called a chiropractor in. Of course, this helped all these extra doctors out, financially that is. All tests turned out O.K., and poor Claudia was listed to be dismissed the next day. She hadn't even gotten to wear all her new flashy nighties she had bought purposely to lounge around in. She was so disappointed over having to leave so soon that she was unable to sleep all night. Guess what? Old Claudia had one tenth degree of fever the next morning, and her doctor found a reason to rake in a little more dough. This time she was given oxygen, I.V.'s, and even put her in traction.

Claudia persuaded the male nurse to let her put another pair of her new pajamas on, which he did. After she was all prettied up, she called all her relatives and friends about her fever and told them it could be possible she could take pneumonia, asking them to please let the preacher know. Brother Biggs was the new, good looking, young, single man that had just taken over the pastorate of Claudia's church. He came right over and Claudia tried her sick stuff. She tried coughing pretending to be hoarse, she had practiced on that before and could do a bang-up job of it. She rubbed her chest as if it was hurting. Brother Biggs had a short conversation with her, said it was best to not talk too much, bade her good-bye and left. He knew then that Claudia would not be on his list as a candidate for minister's wife.

When the doctor checked her temperature, the one-tenth degree was long gone. There was no more hospital stay for Claudia and no more cash for the doctor. Claudia very reluctantly packed her three new sets of sleepwear still in the bags they came in. Oh, well. Why worry? It wouldn't be long until some more pains would pop up.

Claudia was feeling fine after she got home and unpacked her clothes. Tonight was the big college football game and Fred her boyfriend had just called and had bought two tickets at half price from someone who couldn't make it to the game. Claudia really cared for Fred for he sympathized with her for all the illnesses she came up with. Claudia accepted the invitation and was happy to be able to get to go. (Sometimes its very rewarding to not be playing sick.) The ball game was very exciting with the home team winning 18 to 13 points. Claudia was so thrilled being with Fred and seeing all the people, plus the victory, she hadn't realized how hard the seats were, and after the game was over, it had happened again: the dreadful pain in her left hip. Fred had to almost carry her out of the bleachers. After she was comfortably placed in Fred's car and held closely in Fred's arms for some time (she was pretty, very feminine and sexy), Claudia forgot about her hip.

Riding home in Fred's arms was very exciting, and the ride home ended much too soon. Actually having Fred on her mind, caused her hip pain to fly away and Claudia only thought of romance and maybe a proposal. She slept through the night without a pain disturbing her peaceful sleep. Life went on as usual for three whole days and Fred hadn't called, and that brought on another hip attack. She called her fee-grabber doctor again and explained how the excruciating pains were shooting through her hip and down her leg. The doctor comforted her by telling her to report to the hospital immediately, for there was danger of the pain becoming so severe she could easily have convulsions. Claudia took time to call her friends and asked them to get the news circulating over the neighborhood. She even called Fred and told him about her serious illness. Fred promised her he'd send her roses and would come to see her as soon as she was able to have company. That pleased Claudia so much she almost forgot about her serious hip attack.

Fred finally dropped in to see Claudia, but, much to her disappointment, the doctor had taken her out of traction, which she didn't need to begin with. She had to tell him she was scheduled to go home tomorrow. This left Fred with very little sympathy for her. He did kiss her a little in the presence of a nurse and patted her face and ran his fingers through her hair. He told her he hoped she soon recovered, so they could take a little cruise on the General Jackson. That put color in Claudia's cheeks, and she gathered up her belongings and had him take her home. She had had a miraculous hip healing experience.

The trip on the General Jackson was a romantic experience, causing her to forget about her high 1/10 degree of fever and hip ache. In fact, all she thought of as they cruised up the river was Fred and the romantic behavior he was so lavishly bestowing on her.

The trip soon ended, and after she was safely home it dawned on her how stuffy her nose was and she had pains developing in her shoulders and chest. She blamed it on the fog on the river. After all Fred did squeeze her pretty strongly. This time when she entered the hospital the doctor found she had two broken ribs, five vertebrates dislocated and cramps in her lower abdomen. Fred really put out on that trip, both physically and financially. He had bought her some Garth Brooks, Allen Jackson and George Jones tapes, and looked for one of Elvis Presley's, but someone in front of him got the last one of Elvis's. About the physical put out, he just got overjoyed and squeezed Claudia ten degrees too hard, breaking her ribs and vertebrates. She really needed the hospital staff this time. Even the preacher was needed, and Fred spent much time with her, feeling just a little embarrassed over his uncontrollable strength.

With all the cards, flowers and visits Claudia received this time, she realized how stupid she had been. She soon recovered, married Fred, and never even wants to talk about her illness. Sometimes love plays tricks; that is, if you take it seriously. After all, who likes to play sick, when there's so much to do to be happy and love and be loved?

It cured Claudia, it can cure you and it's much more enjoyable than a dose of nerve medicine, or a tenth degree of fever, or broken vertebrates! Thanks for reading this!

So long!

See ya!

PHEASANT DRIVE

With tear-filled eyes, Cliff glanced in the rear view mirror for the last time at the big old house that was home for eight years. Soon he was out of sight with only the memories he would treasure forever.

He had carefully packed the van with things he would need to start a new life. Miles sped by and soon he was out of Massachusetts. Cliff barely knew where he was going, he knew only that it was somewhere in northwestern Colorado. Uncle Clay had seen Cliff's marriage crumbling, and having a cabin ten miles north east of Lafayette, Colorado, he gave it to Cliff, the cabin and four acres of land that went with it. Clay knew he was getting too old to take any more hunting trips. It was now legally Cliff's even if he didn't have any sense of direction except a worn map Uncle Clay had given him with the deed. The trip was long, lonely, and very tiresome, with the crippled leg Cliff had the misfortune to get while he was in the Korean war. Cliff managed to drive a certain number of miles each day with throbbing pains in his leg.

Cliff was a pleasant intelligent man, with a heart full of kindness and love for everyone. He had gotten a medical discharge from the service prior to the close of the war. After coming back home, things were different from what they were before he went to war.

Moureen was not the bride he had married eight years earlier. He had no way of pleasing her. The more he tried to please her the more it seemed to irritate her. She always had interests contrary to what he liked to do. He couldn't take her dancing anymore, for his crippled leg just wouldn't bend like it once did. The business she owned seemed to take her away from home too much, and she always came home very temperamental and fussy with Cliff, even fussy with their five-year-old son Cliff Jr. Moureen was a daddy's girl and visited her parents in Hartford, Connecticut, quite often, never inviting Cliff to come along. After coming back she always had a colder attitude toward him, even blaming him for things he never thought of doing. All these things kept Cliff's mind busy as he drove along. After seemingly endless days Cliff saw a sign which read, "Two miles to Lafayette Colo." The sign was pointing northwest. By now he had the worn yellow page of directions memorized.

When he reached Lafayette, he was tired and very hungry. Seeing a restaurant called "Long Horn," he pulled in and got out. Cindy, the head waitress, welcomed him with a big western grin and asked him as many questions as he cared to answer, then took his order. After eating a large steak and a baked potato and washing it down with strong black coffee, he felt much better. He was interested now in finding the post office, a bank, and a grocery store.

An old gentleman was close by and Cliff asked him for directions. The old man looked him in the eye and asked, "Air ye frum aroun heir?" Cliff with his Boston accent finally made him understand why he was asking questions. Cindy overheard the conversation and took time away from other guests to tell him where everything in the town could be found. Cliff offered no sign of flirtation, thanked her, and left the restaurant.

He headed for the post office, rented a box, then went to the bank to make a deposit and to be recognized as a patron. After getting business straightened out, he found a grocery store and bought everything he thought he would be needing. The van was filled to the top, but he saved room for one ten-gallon can of kerosene. He filled up with gasoline, then got the ten-gallon can filled. He crawled in his van with barely room to drive. He remembered Uncle Clay telling him there were no electrical lines for miles from his cabin.

It was getting around two o'clock in the afternoon on September 25, and the days were getting shorter and cold. Cliff knew he must hurry and find Pheasant Drive before dark. Leaving the small town of Lafayette, he headed north again, taking exit 35, not knowing where he might end up. Uncle Clay told him that when he reached the fork of a road, he'd see a small sign saying "Pheasant Drive" (Uncle Clay said he put it there himself), and he would go left, with Deer Lodge to the right. Uncle Clay cautioned him to be sure and take Pheasant Drive and that would lead him to the cabin. "Two miles up the drive," Uncle Clay had said, "look to your right, and off the road a little way is a cabin. Just keep going two more miles and then you'll come to what is your cabin."

Looking at the so-called road, he could hardly call it that, but he had to try. He found out to not press the gas peddle down too far. There were rocks and holes so full of leaves that the drive was covered and he was unable to see what was under them. The two miles came and he looked for the cabin; glancing to his right he got a glimpse of it. He couldn't look for long for he needed to be seeing all he could see. He kept watching the odometer, wanting to see the next two miles come up. Suddenly a deer with big antlers running across the road almost caused him to wreck. As he drove by, pheasants were disturbed and started making their calls. Cliff wondered if anyone lived in the first cabin, maybe a trapper, a gold digger, or maybe someone like him, living there seeking refuge.

The further he drove the more exhausted he became, wondering why fate had played such a dirty trick on him. Then his mind raced back to Boston and he wondered about Cliff Jr. and Moureen. All at once he saw the cabin.

Getting out of the van he walked up to the cabin and fumbled for the key Uncle Clay had given him, and found it in his pocket. Uncle Clay had tied it to a piece of thin wood with a red cord on it so it would be easier to find. Cliff thought, 'Now if this is the right key, I'll be okay. Putting it in the key hole, feeling better than he had felt in some time, he called out, "Hey anybody home?" Only his echo came back, and he walked in, looking over his haven of peace.

There were only two rooms, the living room and kitchen combined in an 18 foot by 20 foot room, and the bedroom was 10-foot by 12-foot. There was a wood heating stove, which was used for cooking; it was wide and long enough that three pots could be used at once. It also had a chimney over which Uncle Clay had put a piece of plywood to keep birds and animals out of the house while he was away.

The house was not overly furnished. The kitchen furniture consisted of the stove, a homemade eating table, and two straight cane bottom chairs (very dusty); on one side of the wall were shelves and on the north end of the room was a closet. His bedroom was furnished with one old bed with springs (Uncle Clay had told him to bring a mattress for he had burned his before he left; it had become knotty and musty) and one small table. The house was dusty and smelled of mold. Cliff got busy unloading his van, first unloading the mattress. It was hard for a crippled man to unload a mattress, but after all he had put it in by himself. After getting everything moved in, he noticed it was getting dusky outside. Remembering Uncle Clay saying there was a stream near the house that would furnish him with water, he looked through boxes hurriedly and found a bucket. Rushing out to find the stream, he was surprised to find it so near the house. Returning to the house, Cliff saw a rick of wood stacked near the house, and a stack on the small front porch.

Cliff built a fire in the stove; he knew it was his job from now on to cook his meals. As the stove was heating Cliff hunted for his lamps, finally found them, and filled them with oil. By then it was time they were lit.

Cliff was wanting coffee, and he finally found a pot Uncle Clay had left. Washing it out with soapy water he made a full pot. He found his can opener and opened up a can of pork and beans and warmed them up on the stove. The table was dusty and Cliff found a sponge and gave it a good cleaning. He was hungry and it was time to eat; to him pork and beans, slices of bread, and hot coffee had never tasted so good. In fact it was so good he ate the whole can of beans. Before he ate, he took time to thank God for all the many blessings he had given him since he left Boston. He had had a safe trip and found his haven without much trouble. He asked God to watch over Moureen and Cliff Jr. Feeling full and satisfied he sat back in a lounge chair he had brought along and listened to the voices of the wild animals and birds, which would become his friends, and thought that maybe he would learn their language.

Dropping off to sleep, he dreamed of little Cliff Jr. playing around his feet and Moureen telling the boy to watch his manners. Suddenly he was awakened by a thump on the door. He knew he must be cautious in opening it. He shone his flashlight through the window, and the light flashed on a big black bear. The door was heavy and he knew the bear couldn't break through. He put it in his diary, that his first visitor in Pheasant Drive was a big black bear that he didn't even invite in.

It was getting late and Cliff was worn out and ready for bed. After putting sheets and blankets on the bed, he turned in to sleep his first night in his new home in high country. The night became cold, and the heat from the stove soon cooled down. Cliff awakened and, feeling chilled, he remembered he had brought more blankets and comforters. Searching for his flashlight and finding it, he opened boxes until he found more covers. The clock it showed only 2:00 a.m. While he lay shivering, thoughts ran through his mind of all the conveniences he had left in Boston. All the things he had left were for Moureen and Cliff Jr., and all he wanted now was for their happiness.

Moureen didn't want a divorce, although Cliff would have given her one to make her happy. All she wanted (she thought) was Cliff out of her sight and to have Cliff Jr. as hers only. He thought of how they had divided the property, and how he had left plenty for her and Cliff Jr. Bringing his personal belongings and his share of money, he knew there would be many things to buy, plus repairs for the house, and the upkeep of his van. He didn't know at the time what an asset his van would be, driving over the bumpy road he had to travel over. He knew he must be careful with his money even if he did draw a big disabled veteran captain's check. He was glad Moureen didn't know where he was going–it was best that way. The question arose as to how could he keep in touch with Cliff Jr. So many questions without answers ran through his mind. Hours later Cliff fell asleep and slept until the sun was high above the fir trees outside his small window. Dreading to put his feet on the cold floor, he finally ventured out of the warm bed.

Cliff needed practice building fires, but he finally got one going. Soon the room was nice and warm, and after warming last night's coffee, he was soon drinking it down. He then made a fresh pot. He read the directions on a bag of pancake mix and tried his luck at making them, going strictly by directions, and much to his surprise, they turned out delicious, tasting just like his mom's used to taste. After finishing his breakfast, washing his dishes, and getting the house nice and warm, he started unpacking boxes he had brought along. One box in particular caught his eye. He hadn't remembered packing a box with green labels on it. When he opened it, tears filled his eyes, and he saw then that Moureen hadn't wanted him to leave as much as she pretended. Inside the box was a framed picture of the three of them, made two years ago, and another one of their wedding. On down in the box were things she knew he would need, things men never think of needing. She had even put a small box of needles, thread, buttons, and scissors, a wool scarf toboggan and wool socks, which she knew he had overlooked. "How did she know I was going to another cold place like Boston?" he wondered.

He stopped opening boxes and cleaned off the shelves in the living room and sat the pictures where he could see them, asking himself, "Why am I doing this? I came here to try and forget and be forgotten."

Another job Cliff needed to take care of was opening up the fireplace. He took off the piece of plywood that Clay had used to board it up. Time to have fire in the fireplace.

Cliff found another bucket and started to the clear, cool stream for water. After looking over his cabin and four acres of land, mostly in fir, with some white trunked aspen and spruce, he felt a sense of security as he dipped up two buckets of water and returned to the house, being ever watchful for the big brown bear that had paid him an early visit.

The house was beginning to look and feel a little like home. The few dishes and pans he had brought along had been washed and put on the shelves he had just cleaned. His clothes had been hung neatly in the closet. After finding two new matching dish towels Cliff hung them up at the window.

A few weeks later Cliff's wood was getting low, and he knew he must cut a tree and saw it up before colder weather came. He had problems getting his power saw started but managed to get a pole pine cut down. Being close to the house made it very convenient for him. Just as he got the tree cut down he ran out of gas. Tomorrow he would make a trip into town for a tank of gas, pick up his mail, and get milk and bread. He got up early and wrote Uncle Clay, telling him about his trip out west and how he was getting adjusted to a new life in the wild and making sure to tell him who his first and only visitor was, the bear. He then reminded his uncle to keep it quiet where he was, in case the news got out and Moureen found out. "But Uncle Clay," he wrote, "please tell me everything you hear about Cliff Jr." He was careful to not let Uncle Clay know about his feelings for Moureen.

As Cliff was driving into town he made a mental list of things to pick up. Somehow it was enjoyable, living in peace and quiet. He remembered to measure the door size so he could buy a storm door. He wanted it for two purposes: first, so he could look through the door and watch the animals, and second, to help keep the cold winter wind out.

His first stop in town was the post office to mail Uncle Clay's letter and check to see if he had gotten any mail. After picking up a few pieces he went to the bank to make sure the transfer of money had gone through. It had, and now he was ready to shop. First he bought the door, which had to be tied on the top of his van. He also bought nails and a hand saw. Then he went to WalMart and bought two rugs, including a 4 by 6-foot one to go in front of his bed. He saw curtains he liked and bought two sets, one for each room, then he bought a checked plastic table cloth. He bought more dish towels, pot holders, and an extra pan to wash dishes in. He was beginning to feel like a child at Christmas, wanting everything he saw.

After going to the grocery store and buying things (for he had been told to not run short, since you couldn't rely on Colorado weather), he got gas for his saw and car and kerosene for the lamps, and he headed back to his haven on Pheasant Drive. As he passed the cabin on his way home, he thought he got a glimpse of a person, or was it an illusion?

After climbing the rutty hill and unloading the van, he was very proud of his purchases. First he hung the curtains with the curtain rods he bought. He was glad he had bought the curtains, for the dish towels did look out of place and he needed them to wash dishes with anyway. Next he put the rugs down, adding to the coziness of the house. After that he put the checked table cloth on the table. He had it uneven, but he thought it looked fine. All it needed was a woman's touch, but where was the woman? Cliff could have used more water, but that involved getting out after dark, with a bear for a neighbor.

After eating instant potatoes and canned turnip greens, Cliff sat on his folding chair and read the few pieces of mail he picked up at the Post Office. The fire was burning, red embers sparkling, and, with a hypnotized feeling, Cliff found himself seeing different kinds of forms and images. Battles he had been in during the war, hospital rooms, dancing with Moureen, and seeing Cliff Jr. for the first time. What a time to relive the past. After all he had experienced he realized it was time to massage his leg and go to bed.

Waking up early, Cliff got up, cooked breakfast and was anxious to hang the storm door he had bought the day before. It was a tiresome job for one man to do, especially with a crippled leg. After getting it hung he stepped in the house and took a good look at all the beauty that lay in the distance. He saw all kinds of wild animals now: birds, grouse, sage chickens, ring-necked pheasants, quail, occasionally a herd of mule deer as they pranced through the thickets of fir trees, elk, and mountain goats. Being able to see all this in real life was much better than watching anything on television. He could hear the news on his battery radio and watch for animals at the same time.

Thanksgiving was drawing near, and Cliff kept wondering about the neighbor two miles down the road. Taking his gun and ammunition (he was afraid of seeing the bear again) he started hobbling along on his crippled leg the two miles, to check and see if there was a neighbor or not. Coming up to the cabin, he was hesitant about even checking. Picking up the nerve he still had from his war days, he knocked on the door, hoping for someone to open the door. His heart was pounding as if he had been running a race.

Knocking the second time, he heard footsteps, and a voice from inside called out, "Who's there?"

"Clifton Kerr," he answered. The door swung open to a man with gray streaks in his hair and a serious look in his eyes who stood speechless. After getting hold of himself, he almost shouted, "You can't be Cliff Kerr."

"Yeah, but I am, and you must be James Runyon! How fate has thrown us together again! After all these years we've been separated, we meet again on a peaceful lonely mountain."

"Come on in Cliff and tell me all about yourself. Tell me what you've been doing since Korea."

Each one told their life stories. They had fought in the Korean war together, on the same battlefield. Cliff told James all about his son and his marriage breaking up, and after listening, James told of his breakup with Betty. Both had sad endings to their stories. James told of how he was wounded and had gotten a medical discharge. The sun was getting low and Cliff knew he must get back before dark.

Cliff left feeling much better than he had before he came. James felt the same way. They both had gotten things off their chest that had been painful for a long time. Before Cliff left he invited James up to his house for Thanksgiving dinner. James accepted the invitation quickly. He had seen very few people since he had been there except for a forest ranger or a hunter who had got lost from his party. He seldom went into town and made the trips hurriedly, buying groceries, picking up mail, occasionally eating at the Long Horn, and maybe attending a movie at the only theater in Lafayette.

Cliff was excited about cooking a Thanksgiving dinner for an old friend, now his only neighbor. He wanted something traditional in the meat line. Getting his gun, he went into the woods, not knowing what to expect. He would have liked to have killed a wild turkey but would be satisfied with grouse, pheasant, or even a deer. Luckily he got a pheasant. Picking feathers from a fowl was a new experience, but he remembered to put the bird in hot water so the feathers could be plucked out easier. His grandmother used to say feathers could be lain out, dried and used to stuff pillows, he decided he would try saving the softer ones. It was his choice and he had no one to object to his decisions. He had no choice but to cook the pheasant in a pot on the stove, since he didn't have an oven.

James came early, barely making it up the road, which was muddy and rutty, in his jeep. It was such a thrill for Cliff to be able to cook a meal for someone. He sat the table as near to perfection as he knew how and could rememberHe had no china, silver tableware, or crystal glasses, and the table itself was covered with the blue-checked plastic he had bought recently. The meal was finally finished with a varied menu: boiled pheasant (almost too salty), stovetop dressing, cranberry sauce, instant mashed potatoes, canned green beans, already-baked rolls, coffee, and pumpkin pie. James complimented Cliff on the feast and told him he had done an excellent job preparing it, and after living alone for so long, he really did find it delicious. He spent a few more hours with Cliff and left for the treacherous two miles back to his cabin. Each one was thankful he had found the other.

The weather in Colorado changes quickly, and when Cliff got out of bed the next morning he pushed the curtain back and looked out to see a white wonderland–eight inches of snow had fallen since James left last night. Cliff was thankful the snow hadn't come earlier, but since he was snowbound decided he should write Uncle Clay again so that he could mailthe letter the next time he went into town. He wanted to remind him again to find out all he could about Cliff Jr. He would have liked to have added Moureen's name too but didn't dare. Here it was November 25th and he had left Boston September 12th. It already seemed like a year or more had passed by.

The snow was still falling with flakes as big as cigarette papers. The spruce trees looked like pictures an expert artist would paint. As he was watching the snow fall, a herd of mule deer came prancing through the yard. Cliff glanced around on his porch and was happy he had it almost stacked to the top with wood. Looking up, he saw a covey of grouse come fluttering by hunting for something to eat.

Cliff got the fire burning and soon had hot coffee; he warmed up the pheasant left from yesterday and decided to try his luck at making gravy. Something went wrong and it didn't taste like mom used to make it. He had much to learn in cooking, but experience is the best teacher, so he told himself maybe his gravy would be better by next Thanksgiving.

It was very cold in Connecticut, and the snow was coming down in sheets, carrying millions of fluffy snow flakes. The weather reporters gave reports of a heavy snow storm hitting near Hartford, Connecticut, and going on down east to Boston. Weather reporters were urging people to stay off the roads as much as possible.

In Boston the telephone rang and Cliff Jr. answered. His grandmother Josephine Harding told him with sobs in her voice to get his mother on the line at once. Cliff Jr. called Moureen and when she answered a trembling voice told her to come home at once, that her father had had a heart attack and had died half an hour ago. Moureen told her mother the roads were almost impossible to travel over and she would be afraid to try to drive. Josephine insisted that she try to get there; couldn't she find someone to drive her?

Moureen knew now just how much she missed Cliff. Thinking it over, she knew how her parents disliked Cliff and never wanted him around. Dismissing the thought, she decided maybe she could get her friend Walter to drive her and Cliff Jr. to Hartford. Her parents had always wanted her to marry Walter anyway. Moureen's mind was running back to her father and how she was always his favorite child. She always got the biggest apple, the biggest piece of pie, and the biggest hug. In her father's eye no man was good enough for her. If he had chosen one, it would have been Walter, and Moureen understood now, after it was too late, that this was why Cliff was dirt to her parents.

With much sliding and treacherous driving Walter got them there. Mom was delighted to see Walter, even in the midst of her trouble, hoping there might be hopes of them marrying. The snow became deeper, but friends made it to their home, offering sympathy and carrying in food. Moureen's brother and sister and their families were there too. Something in Moureen's heart caused her to miss Cliff more than she missed her father, now that they were both gone. She wondered what caused her to have feelings like that at a time like this.

The snow passed on down east, and the weather became bearable for the funeral. Mr. Harding was a well-known businessman, known by a majority of the people in Hartford, and hundreds turned out for the funeral. Moureen had to get back to carry on her business and Cliff Jr. had to get back to school. As for Walter, it didn't make any difference; he was from a wealthy family and never had to work. The roads were clear and they made better time getting back home.

Mrs. Harding seemed to adjust quickly to losing her husband. She was a very haughty, independent woman, almost despicable at times. She took time off from all the business she had to take care of (for she didn't trust her son Jake or her other daughter Alice) to come to Boston to visit Moureen. Something told Moureen her mother was coming for something more than to pay her a visit. "Could she be trying to light a fire between me and Walter?' Moureen wondered. 'If that's why she's here she can forget it."

Mom seemed to be enjoying herself until she saw Cliff's picture sitting on Moureen's dresser in her bedroom. She pitched a big fit and threatened to throw it in the waste can. Moureen soon convinced her mother it was best to not do it, for she was learning real fast what her and Cliff's trouble was: she just listened too much to her parents. She thought of what a wonderful husband Cliff had been and how horribly she had treated him. She was remembering now how each time she visited her parents she came home having more problems with Cliff. She thought again, "It wasn't Cliff, it was me, yes me, being influenced by my parents. I drove away the only man I can ever love."

Josephine was missing Jake more every day and taking it out on Moureen, by accusing her of being in contact with Cliff. Moureen would not admit to her mother that she had no earthly idea where Cliff was. Deep in her heart she would give anything to hear his voice again. Josephine stayed a few more days and then returned home.

Moureen spent time with her mother when it was convenient, but seeing things differently now, she didn't go home nearly so often as she did when her father was alive.

Cliff Jr. was growing up and getting involved in many school activities, keeping Moureen busy with caring for him and keeping her business in order. Sometimes it seemed as if she could not endure it any longer. It had been three long years since she had told Cliff to get out of her life and he had left. He had always seen to keeping repair jobs done around the house. He hadn't let coming back from the service with a wounded leg stop him from keeping things repaired, and he never complained at mean things she would say. All these things kept running through her mind.

James picked up Cliff's mail at the post office and brought it up to him. Cliff was in much pain; he had twisted his injured leg as he was trying to plant some seed in his small garden. James took out his mail and started reading it, as Cliff fumbled through his. The Colorado weather was beautiful and the days were warm enough to sit on the tiny porch and watch for birds and animals that came by often.

James rose out of his chair and told Cliff in an excited tone that he had to get home, pack a bag, and head east. Cliff looked up from reading his mail and asked why; "Not going to stay, I hope."

"Oh, no, no. Just got a letter telling me to come to Fred's–my brother's. There's some business I've got to see about," James said. "Take care of that leg so it will be better and we can go hunting this fall."

"I'll be missing you, James," said Cliff. "Check on Cliff Jr. if you have half a chance to." James went bouncing down the road and was soon out of sight. Cliff felt very lonely having his only friend and neighbor leave.

James left early the next morning, not knowing when he could catch a plane. After he got on a paved road the time went by quickly, and he wondered when he got to Denver what to expect then. He was also thinking what might be expected of him when he got to Fred's. He hadn't bothered to do much explaining; all he said was, "Come as quick as you can." After getting to Denver, James checked on planes leaving for Hartford. He had just missed the last flight out. All he could do was wait until early the next day. He was tired and hungry. After eating a meal in a restaurant, he went to the airport and picked up his ticket. Checking in a motel, he had a bath, dressed, and went out for supper. He asked the motel attendant to wake him at 6:15 a.m., then went to his room and turned in.

The call came much too soon the next morning. James rubbed his eyes and tried to get them opened, almost wishing he were back on Pheasant Drive in his humble little cabin. After taking a shower and having breakfast, James wondered if his jeep would make it to the airport, and luckily it did. James boarded the plane with his battered suitcase and clothes that weren't Connecticut-style.

Hours passed and James was enjoying the trip and wondering how things were back home. He had failed to keep in close contact with his brother Fred. Betty, an old girlfriend, had turned him down when he came back from service, and all he ever wanted, he thought, was to forget it all. He knew he could never stand to see her with another man or having children that should be his. He was so engrossed in his feelings, he found himself talking aloud. An old bald-headed man sitting on the other side of the plane gave him a stern look as if he thought he might be a little off and drew James' attention. At the same time, the plane became bumpy and James was awakened from the thoughts he had been imprisoned with for many years.

After changing planes in Kansas City, Missouri, and heading east again, James fell into a deep sleep and slept until the plane was taxing into the airport in Hartford. James awakened and, getting off the plane, headed for his luggage. Waiting for his battered old suitcase to make its turn around, he was wondering who he might see first that he knew. No one seemed to notice him as he walked to the front of the station to catch a cab. As he opened the door, the cab driver asked, "Where to?" James said, "Take me to 212 Green Briar Avenue." "Yes, sir," replied the driver.

In a short time James was ringing the doorbell at his brother's home. A little four-year-old girl with long blonde curly hair came to the door. Seeing he was a stranger, she screamed for her mommy. As Paula came to the door she recognized James, and tears streamed down her cheeks as she embraced him.

"James, it's been so long since you've been here. Fred will be home soon and he will be so happy to see you. Did you get Fred's letter?" she said.

"Yes, I got it day before yesterday. I don't go into town for my mail very often," he answered.

"Fred was expecting you earlier, but he'll understand."

James seemed very puzzled over what Paula had said. She saw the expression on James' face and told him, "Maybe things could be changed."

Paula told James to meet the little niece he had never seen before. Paula told Mary Anne, "This is your only uncle James, whom you have never seen." Little Mary Ann came up to her mother looking puzzled and said, "I didn't know I had an uncle." Paula apologized, and told James they had been really careful not to let anyone know where he was, since that was his wish. Speaking before she thought, she said, "People say Betty has never been able to find the right man yet. Dates them for a while and then lets them go. She's never happy with anyone for long. I think she lives in the suburbs of Hartford. We've never met her or seen her as far as we know."

The door opened and Fred came in and, surprised to see James, he became speechless. After regaining his thoughts, he grabbed James and gave him a big hug. "I thought by now the letter must have gotten lost," he said.

James answered, "But I only got it day before yesterday. I got here as quickly as possible. The roads I have to travel are rough and bumpy and hard to get over."

While Fred was washing up and Paula was finishing up supper, James picked up the Hartford Times newspaper, and glancing over the obituaries he noticed Josephine Harding's name listed. The name sounded familiar; "Seems as if I have heard Cliff mention the name," he thought. Reading on he came to the survivors, one son and two daughters, one being Moureen Kerr. The family would be receiving friends tonight from 7 to 9 p.m. He might be able to get information about Cliff Jr.

After eating a delicious meal, James decided to go to the funeral home. He knew he could go and never be identified as a friend of Cliff Kerr.

James' clothes didn't come up to the standards of those worn by the friends of Josephine Harding. Fred couldn't understand why James just had to go, and Fred felt a little out of place going. He didn't know James felt the same way but fully intended to find out all he could about Cliff Jr. As they were viewing the body, James eyes caught sight of a boy that resembled Cliff, and, being with the family, he just had to be Cliff's son. He was so excited his heart was pounding as if it would jump out. In a short while Fred was ready to go home, but James kept wanting to stay.

James saw Cliff Jr. whisper to his mother; like most boys he got tired of being nice and quiet. The woman Cliff Jr. whispered to just had to be Moureen, she looked so much like the picture Cliff had on his shelf, except she had aged and her hair was trimmed in natural gray. As Cliff Jr. started out, James told Fred he was ready to go. Following him out, James asked the boy if he was Cliff Kerr Jr. Looking James in the eye, he asked, "How did you know my name?" James replied, "Oh just a guess, I suppose."

James, wanting to hear him say it again, said, "And you are Cliff Kerr, Jr.?" "Yes," said Cliff Jr. "And that is my grandmother in there." James sympathized and asked if his father was there, just to try to keep down suspicion, and said he would like to speak to him. "Oh no," said Cliff Jr. "Mom asked dad to leave a few years ago, and he did. We don't know where he went. Mom prays for him every night; she says granddaddy and grandmother were the cause of it happening. I wish daddy would come back. If you ever see him tell him we love him."

James and Fred sat up late that night talking about business deals and how the government was making a mess of things. James had only a radio to listen to at home. Finally Fred changed the subject from business and politics and asked James why he was so interested in that lanky boy that belonged to the uppity Harding family. James finally broke down and told the whole story of how Moureen Harding Kerr had asked Cliff to leave, and how he came to be living in a little cabin that belonged to his uncle Clay. "He lives just two miles farther in the wilderness from me," James explained. "My long-lost buddy had unknowingly moved in next door to me." He told Fred how their friendship had grown since living there. They both faced bitter love. Fred knew then that James still had a warm place in his heart for Betty.

Fred called his place of business early the next morning and told his secretary something urgent had come up and to carry on until he got back. The two men quickly dressed and ate breakfast and then rushed to the lawyer's office, where Fred explained to the lawyer why James had been unable to come and sign a paper that had been left for him to inherit a large amount of money from a dear old aunt. As this was the first time James had heard this story, his mouth flew open and stayed that way. Fred explained that he had written him, but James hadn't picked his mail up. The time of signing the paper had barely elapsed. Offering the lawyer more money persuaded him to move the date up and make it legal. James was elated over the inheritance. He never dreamed Aunt Claudia would have Fred and him named in the will. She had always seemed partial to Aunt Myrtle's children.

James stayed with Fred and Paula longer than he planned to, wishing while he was there that he might get at least a glimpse of Betty. Fred and Paula took James out to eat in the Rolls and Roses restaurant the night before James was leaving for home. The waitress seated two women at a table near the Runyons. James looked and knew he must be seeing Betty Blake. She hadn't changed much; she seemed to have mellowed some and didn't seem so haughty; she had a kind, sweet look he had never seen on her before. James glanced at her, never catching her eye. In the meantime Betty was glancing at him. After the Runyons were through eating, James tipped the waitress and the family went home.

In the morning, Fred drove James to the airport, where he barely caught his early flight. As the brothers shook hands, tears filled their eyes. James, trying to speak in a strong voice, invited Fred and his family to come visit him, and Fred promised he would.

James had a nice flight back to Denver without any layovers, which made him happy because he was a nervous flyer and detested layovers. He found his Jeep just as he had left it. After filling up with gas and oil, James was on his long way home. He was very concerned about Cliff and was hoping his friend's leg would be better. On and on he drove until he finally came to the fork of the road where Pheasant Drive turns left.

It was good to be this near home, and he wondered if he should stop at home or go on to Cliff's and check on him. Something told him to keep going, so he climbed the steep slopes to Cliff's house. When he came in sight of the house he didn't see Cliff on the porch where he sat in pretty weather. A lump came up in his throat; he didn't know how to expect finding him. When he turned the motor off and opened his jeep door, he heard Cliff call out, "Come in, James, if that's you." Running inside the cabin, James found Cliff in bed running a fever, with red streaks running up his crippled leg. James didn't ask Cliff if he wanted to see a doctor; he rolled him out of bed, put him in Cliff's van where he could be more comfortable, and rushed down the bumpy road as quickly as possible.

Once he got on the paved road he drove as fast or maybe faster then the laws in Colorado allowed. It was 50 miles from Lafayette to the nearest hospital. Cliff was getting delirious. James was pushing the gas pedal lower and lower, expecting to be stopped by a cop any minute. Looking down at the gas gauge, he found it on empty. James said, "Please God let there be a gas station around this next curve," and to his prayer, there was a station. Pulling in, he jumped out to fill up the tank. The gas ran in slower than it ever had. Finally they were back on the road. He saw a sign which read "5 miles to Takoma Hospital." Cliff had quit making any sounds, and James wondered if he could make it for five more miles.

After arriving at the hospital, James called out, "It 's an emergency!" Doctors and nurses rushed to him and, seeing Cliff's condition, began working to save his life. Infection had set up in his leg and his temperature reached 104 degrees. The doctors didn't give James much hope for the time being. The receptionist was trying to find James so they could get in touch with Cliff's relatives. When she found James by Cliff's side, that told her that James was the only connection he had. The doctors were pretty sure his leg would have to be amputated. They tried new medicines, trying to save his leg. James went home to check on things, put on clean clothes and unpack his suitcase.

James rushed back to the hospital to stay with Cliff as long as he might live. On the seventh day after Cliff had entered the hospital the doctors started having hopes of his recovery. The infection was about gone and Cliff had recognized James. Two days later he ate some food. Gradually, he was gaining his strength back.

One day Cliff looked at James and asked about his trip east. Picking up nerve he asked about Cliff Jr. He was afraid James hadn't made contact. James asked him if he was able to listen. A knot came up in Cliff's throat; thinking James had bad news, he broke into a cold sweat. James told him not to get alarmed, it was good news. He told him he had seen his son in the funeral home where his mother-in-law was, recounting the conversation he had, and told how Cliff Jr. said his mother longed for her husband.

The next morning Cliff was a different man; he ate all his breakfast and asked for more. The doctor was amazed at the sudden change; he told Cliff if he kept improving like he was now, he'd be back home soon, if James would stay with him for a few days. Three days later Cliff was discharged from the hospital. On the way home Cliff had James stop at a store and buy an inflated mattress so he would have it to sleep on. He also had him to buy a good-sized mirror and a small table for the living room and another set of pillows. They stopped again in Lafayette for his medication and groceries.

Everything was different when they got back to Pheasant Drive. They both seemed to have something more to live for than just each other's friendship. Cliff had James tell him all about Cliff Jr. and Betty, never missing hearing the part about Moureen. He was feeling much better and James thought it was time for him to go back home. James left Cliff's house early one Tuesday morning, after seeing that everything was in order. It was good to be back in his own cabin, the place he called home, and to have all the memories he brought back with him from Hartford. He was thinking of Betty and asking himself, "Why didn't I have the nerve to go talk to her? She looked so sweet and humble that if I had drawn her attention, I'm sure things would be better right now. The thorn that stuck in our hearts would have been pulled out and the wound would be healed. I was stubborn and wouldn't make the first move. Now I'm paying for it."

"Well, so much for that," he thought. "It's lunchtime and I don't have much food to choose from. Staying at Cliff's so long has gotten me off schedule." He heated a can of turnip greens, then he fried some corn fritters and made a pot of coffee. It didn't taste too bad, even after all the good food he had gotten while he was in Connecticut.

After James' visit to Connecticut and Cliff's illness and recovery, things changed for the men. They got out and made a few friends. They liked to go to the Long Horn to eat and see people. James drove Cliff's van, for Cliff was told by the doctors to go easy on his leg if he wanted a complete recovery. The bumpy miles seemed to get shorter and easier to travel. On their way to town they brought their laundry to a washerette. Violet was in charge of the washerette and was very helpful with their clothes. She mended them when they needed mending and pressed their shirts and pants. After leaving the washerette they headed for the Long Horn restaurant. The waitresses always wanted to talk.

Cindy, the head waitress, made a point to always serve their table. Chewing her chewing gum and pecking her pencil on their table, she asked questions about where they lived, what they did, and if they had familes. Neither man was anxious to answer, but she asked again, "Where did you say you men lived?" Cliff looked at James and they hesitated, both thinking she wouldn't know where Pheasant Drive was. Finally James said, "We live on Pheasant Drive." Before he hardly had it out of his mouth, she said "Oh, I know where that is. You turn left where the road forks; if you go right it will take you to

Deer Lodge where you ski in the winter time. What's up when you go to Pheasant Drive?" Cindy asked. Not knowing what she meant by saying what's up, they waited again on each other to give her an answer. Cliff raised his eyebrows at James and said, "It's just a road up in the ridges." Each one thought she was getting a little too personal, so they left a tip and got gone in a hurry.

It was still early and the men decided they would check on prices of gas refrigerators and gas stoves. Since James had come into money he was thinking of a modern life again. After checking with the only appliance store in Lafayette, they found what they wanted. The owner only had two small gas stoves and two refrigerators. They wanted them very much but played around with the price tags. Finally the manager told them if they wanted all four pieces they could have them cheaper if they paid cash and he'd reduce the cost of the gas tanks. "One more thing," James said, "You'll have to deliver, since we don't have any way in getting it out to our homes." The merchant scratched his head and thought for a few seconds, and said, "I'll bring them out the first thing in the morning." After they told them where they lived he knew exactly where it was; he had brought the heater out to Clay's a number of years ago. The men got a little more extravagant and they both bought linoleum rugs for their combined living rooms and kitchens. Cliff thought now was the time to buy a comfortable chair since he could have it delivered. The store also carried furniture, and Cliff found a recliner just like he wanted, so he took that too. Looking around they saw two chests of drawers, and they bought them. After the merchant counted it all up, he saw that it was the biggest sale he had made since last Christmas. The salesman thanked the men as they started out and told them they would get their order first thing tomorrow. The men teased each other and said they had more modern furniture and appliances than anyone on Pheasant Drive. Knowing that after tomorrow, they could bake canned biscuits and keep frozen food in their refrigerators, they headed for the grocery store and loaded up there, too.

They went by the washerette and picked up their laundry. Violet was a kind woman and had done up their clothes carefully. There was something about her that could make anyone like her. She was tall and thin with deep brown eyes and thick brown hair combed back and in a bun on the back of her neck. She was a nice lady and could build you up when your life seemed empty. Cliff and James were getting attached to her. Cliff still hung on to Moureen, and James had the same feeling for Betty. Maybe it was the mothering instinct in Violet that gave them the feeling they were having for her.

Moureen, her sister Joyce, and Jake Jr. had worked endlessly trying to get their parents' estate wound up. It had been over six months since their mother died. Moureen went back and forth from Boston to Hartford all this time, trying to keep her business in order and helping to close her parents' estate was more than she could endure.

One day Cliff Jr. said, "Mom, you remember when grandmother died, and we were at the funeral home; I asked you if I could go out. A man followed me out, and asked me if I was Cliff Kerr, Jr. He asked questions, and he seemed concerned. He was with the man that owns the appliance store at Crescent and Oak Street." She asked why he hadn't told her sooner. She questioned how the man looked, and she felt like it wasn't Cliff or she would have recognized him. She could hardly wait until she could go to Hartford. This was the first lead she had on Cliff's whereabouts since he left four years ago. As soon as she solved her problems in her business, she rushed back to Hartford, taking Cliff Jr. with her, thinking he might identify the man who asked him so many questions. This time it was for her own concern and not for the hectic job of settling her mother's estate.

Cliff and James were both up early and ready for the delivery man to bring their prized possessions out to them. It was getting around noon, and the truck hadn't come. Cliff and James were like children looking for Santa Claus. Finally James heard a truck coming up the road. He could hardly wait for it to turn in at his cabin, but instead of turning in, it went on up the ridge to Cliff's. Cliff asked a second favor: would they help lay the rug? After making such a big sale, the men couldn't say no, so Cliff's day turned out very lucky. Cliff paid the men and added a bonus. The men were pleased and thanked Cliff and started down the road to James's: he was a neat housekeeper and in no time he had his cabin looking like a woman had touched it up. Cliff worked all day getting things as he wanted them. He began to see many more things he needed for his house.

James came up and invited Cliff for supper. It was the first time Cliff had been invited to eat with him. James tried his hand at preparing the food and setting the table. He did a good job of opening cans, and both men enjoyed supper: a can of roast beef with gravy, green beans, instant rice, and instant chocolate pudding in a teacup. James tried his new oven out by baking rolls he had bought. he hadn't bothered to put down a tablecloth, and he remembered Cliff had one on his table. James couldn't see why a nice bath towel wouldn't look all right, and since he didn't have a bathroom, he couldn't use the towel after all. Cliff copied James and told him how much he enjoyed the meal. After shooting the breeze a while, Cliff left, inviting James up to eat the next time he went in for groceries, promising him he would serve cooked frozen food. Now that they had refrigerators they could start eating like city folk.

In late September, a cool breeze was stirring the beautiful colored leaves Connecticut trees have every fall. The nippy days and nights assured the people fall was already there. Before getting out of her car, Moureen looked in a mirror and saw deep wrinkles forming in her face. A few streaks of gray could be seen mingled in her shiny black hair. Dabbing on some lipstick and pulling her jacket in place, Moureen walked into the appliance store, having no idea what the name of the man she wanted to speak towas. It was like hunting for a needle in a haystack. She saw a man and recognizing him to be a clerk, she asked, "Excuse me, but did I see you at my mother's funeral six months ago?" He asked who her mother was, and she said, "Josephine Harding." Bells began ringing in Fred's mind, and he remembered being there with James. Moureen asked if his brother wasn't with him. She was only guessing, hoping to get to the bottom of it. Fred said, "Oh, yes. I remember being there with my brother James. May I ask you why you are asking all these questions?"

Moureen said, "Yes, I'll tell you. Your brother questioned my son, asking if his father was Cliff Kerr. My husband has been gone for five years, and I would love to locate him. If you would just tell me where your brother is, then I might be able to locate Cliff. My son needs his father, and as for me, I need him too. I can't call back asking him to leave, and I was wrong."

Fred Runyon said, "I can give you my brother's name. It's James Runyon, and he gets his mail in Lafayette, Colorado. That's about all I can tell you; he said he lived on Pheasant Drive. Lafayette is northeast of Denver." He continued, "I hope I've been of help to you."

Moureen thanked him and told him he'd never know how much he had helped. She and Cliff Jr. started back to the car. The crisp air was so refreshing to Moureen and the information she had just received made her feel like she could fly with just a little help. Moureen didn't go by to check on her brother and sister. She had found what she was searching for, and she headed back to Boston to make plans to finish her investigation.

Betty Blake was nervous and restless. No one seemed to be able to interest her in anything. She was pretty and very popular, but something had happened six months ago that had changed her in so many different ways. She had lost interest in dating men; she was dropping out of all her social activities. Every day since she had seen a face in the Rolls and Roses restaurant, her life had been changed. She felt that she had to find that face. She had rejected him one time and had regretted it ever since. She had heard he had left town, and no one, as far as she could tell, knew of his whereabouts except his brother Fred, and he kept it quiet. She wondered if he had a wife and children. She wondered how things could get any worse between them. Something told her if she went back to the Rolls and Roses restaurant, she might be able to see him again. It was worth a try, and as soon she was being seated, she told the waitress which table she wanted. The waitress hesitated, saying the table she wanted would seat six, but Betty insisted, for that was the table she had been seated at when she saw James before. She seated herself facing the other table just as she had six months ago. She wondered how she could remember the date so well. Because an old love had been rekindled, that's why! Was it a coincidence that the same couple with the little girl came to the same table they had eaten at six months ago? She had heard James speak of his brother Fred. It would be worth a try to casually go to their table and ask if he was James Runyon's brother. "Excuse me, sir. Are you James Runyon's brother?"

"Why yes, I am. Why do you ask?"

"I knew him many years ago, and after I saw you I was almost sure you were his brother. Just where is James now?" she asked. Before Fred realized what he was saying, he told her James was several miles from Lafayette, Colorado. She asked another question: "Where do you go from there?" And again Fred spoke without thinking and said, "Somewhere on Pheasant Drive." At the time he didn't know he was doing James a favor too. Betty thanked Fred and told them to enjoy their food, going back to her table she managed to eat a little food by forcing it down. She tipped the waitress and left.

As Betty passed Fred and Paula's table, Fred told Paula, "There was something familiar about that woman." Paula told him maybe she had bought appliances from him. Fred tried hard for days to place her but never could.

It was getting cold in Colorado. Cliff and James helped each other get their supply of wood. Having gas ranges helped. Now they needed wood only for warming their cabins with their woodstoves. They were both considering getting coal to burn if they could get it delivered. It would have to be brought in when the road was frozen hard. A heavy load of coal could be delivered over their road only in dry or frozen weather.

Both men were improving in their cooking, and having refrigerators and stoves made it much easier for them. Their biggest dread now was the rutty road in bad weather. Cliff's leg was much better, and he was almost out of pain, except when he stood on it too long. He was really careful when he walked to keep from stepping in holes where animals had dug.

Colorado snows were already falling, and ski slopes were being opened to the skiers. Deer Lodge was open now, and skiers were crowding in from different locations. Most all the reservations in the lodges were taken. At one of the lodges a girl at the desk answered the telephone and a woman with a Boston accent asked if she had a double room. The girl answered with her western accent and said she had one left and the woman took it. Before the desk clerk had time for another sip of coffee the telephone rang again. This time a woman with an accent asked about a room. The desk clerk, with a mouth full of coffee, said, "I'm sorry. A woman from Boston got the last one just a minute ago, but I might have a cancellation for the roads are getting dangerous. We're getting so much snow." Checking her list, she told the woman she had one more room, but it wasn't too cozy. Not knowing what to expect, the woman took it anyway.

It wasn't easy making connections from Boston and Connecticut to a ski resort in Colorado. The planes were loaded and the terrible weather caused layovers. Some stops were delayed by rain and sleet, but snow was the big problem. Moureen and Cliff Jr. had a four-hour layover in St. Louis. They were getting tired and Cliff Jr. asked his mother why they were going to Deer Lodge to ski when he had no desire to ski and he had never heard his mother speak of skiing. Moureen tried to convince him just how much fun they could have skiing on Colorado slopes, but he had no desire to even try skiing.

Finally the plane made it to Denver, where it was able to land. Everyone was rushing off the plane to grab their luggage. Moureen was as anxious as anyone there, maybe just a little more than most of them. The wind was blowing briskly, almost cutting through the heavy jackets and overcoats people were wearing. Finally a bus pulled up and stopped. Moureen asked, without having any sense of direction, if it was going to Lafayette. "Yes, ma'am," replied the driver, so, fumbling for money, she bought two tickets. The bus was crowded with people, mostly skiers heading for Deer Lodge. The road was very icy and dangerous. The driver lost control and almost overturned. Moureen asked the driver how far it was to Lafayette and he said, "My bus registers fifty miles." Moureen was getting more excited every minute and was wondering how they would be able to get to the ski resort. After all, others were heading in that direction, for she had overheard them talking.

After a long, tiresome bus ride, the driver pulled up in front of the Long Horn restaurant. The driver called out, "You are now in Lafayette." Most everyone jumped up, scrambled for the door, grabbed their luggage, and headed inside the Long Horn. The driver said, "We'll only have a twenty-minute rest stop." Only a few long-haired men with guitars were left in the bus, and they made no effort to get out. People rushed into the restaurant. Some used the rest rooms while others were getting seated at tables.

Moureen and Cliff Jr. found a table and waited for a waitress. Cindy, the head waitress, finally came around, talkative as ever. When she asked for the order, Cliff Jr. was slow as usual in making up his mind. Finally Moureen said, "Cliff Jr., give her your order; she's very busy." Cindy's eyes flashed at Moureen and she said, "Did you say Cliff?" Moureen said, "Yes, why?" Cindy said, "Oh well, the name sounds familiar. Two men come in here to eat occasionally from the ski country, and one of them goes by Cliff."

Moureen almost fainted, but after she was able to speak she asked Cindy if she knew where they lived. Pretending to know, Cindy said, "Yeah I think they live on Pheasant Drive. That's left of Deer Lodge, and Deer Lodge is where everybody comes to ski." Moureen didn't want to show too much interest but asked, "How do you get there?" Cindy, acting important, said, "Take exit 35, which will take you northeast. When you come to a fork in the road, one sign turning right will lead you to Deer Lodge, where you go to ski. Then the left side of the road is Pheasant Drive. There used to be a little homemade sign stuck up there, but I don't know if it's still there or not. You know what, I wasn't trying to eavesdrop or anything but I overheard those two men talking one day about Pheasant Drive, and they seemed very secretive about it. When I asked them if they lived there, you know what–they just looked at each other, left me a tip (now they always give good tips), and do you know they left immediately? Even if one of the men is crippled, they got out in a hurry. They rushed out as if they thought I might try to follow them." Moureen played it cool, but everything Cindy said had sunk in.

Moureen called a cab that was in need of much repair. After making the driver understand her Boston accent, she told him to take her to Pheasant Drive. Shaking his head he said he had been to Deer Lodge a number of times but he had never been to Pheasant Drive. Moureen asked, "But you will try, won't you?" Finally he said, "I will if you 're willing to pay a bigger fare." Moureen knew she was going to see Cliff one way or the other. She said, "I'm willing to pay extra, just step on it." She was hoping to find the place before dark. Gerald, the cab driver, told them he might not be able to get them there, but he'd try. Cliff Jr. asked his Mom, "Why are we going out there?" By then they were at the forks of the road, where a small homemade sign read, "Pheasant Drive" just as Cindy said it would. Gerald said, "Here we are. Are you ready for a bumpy road? Or you might have to walk. The roads get bad out here." Moureen was getting more excited each minute. They knew from the tire ruts someone had been driving over the road. It seemed like hours when James' cabin came into sight. Moureen was so ecstatic that she asked Gerald to drive off the road to the cabin. Her heart was in her mouth. As soon as the car stopped, Moureen rushed to the door and knocked, hoping Cliff would open the door, but a man with an unfamiliar face appeared instead. Her disappointment showing in her face, Moureen introduced herself and asked if he might know a man by the name of Cliff Kerr.

Before James answered, he looked her over carefully and asked, "Could you by any chance be Moureen Kerr?" "Yes, I am Moureen Kerr. Could you tell me where I might find Cliff Kerr?" "Yes, he lives farther up on the ridge. We're close friends. In fact, it's two bumpy miles to his cabin. I'm afraid the cab can't make it up there in this weather." Moureen looked distraught and said, "What can my son and I do? I must see Cliff!" James told her to pay the cab driver and he would take them in his jeep. James had bought a new jeep two weeks before, much bigger than the one he'd had. Moureen gave the cab driver a whopper of a tip, thanked him, and wished him good luck in getting back to town. It was a rough, bumpy ride and Cliff Jr. was tired and fussy. The conversation between James and Moureen was mostly on the road and the weather. Moureen wanted news about Cliff. James turned the last curve and Moureen saw a cabin. Fumbling for words, she asked if that was Cliff's cabin. James said, "Yes, I hope you won't be disappointed." But to Moureen it was the most beautiful spot in the world. As James parked the jeep, a herd of deer went prancing between the jeep and the cabin. James was keeping his joy for Cliff hidden by tapping his horn. Cliff came to the door, saw James' jeep, and motioned for him to come on in. But James yelled, "Come on out here. I've got something to show you." As Cliff came up to the jeep, Moureen opened the door and fell in his arms, hoping for forgiveness. Cliff Jr. was speechless; he ran to his father and hugged him as tightly as his little arms would let him. There were more tears shed than snow flakes that were falling–it was a blissful reunion. Moureen looked at Cliff's cabin and knew it was the most beautiful place on earth. It didn't have carpet, electricity, stuffed couches, or mahogany furniture, but it had what she had been missing since Cliff pulled out of her driveway so long ago. Cliff couldn't imagine the big change a few years had made in Cliff Jr.

James wanted to ask about Betty but didn't have the nerve. As he turned the jeep around and headed for home he was thinking how well he would like to relive a fairy tale like the one Cliff was experiencing.

Cliff prepared supper while Cliff Jr. and Moureen took turns using the outside toilet. Cliff was sure to warn them to watch for bears. Before supper Moureen and Cliff Jr. had a nice face and hand bath using the wash pan with heated water from a tea kettle. They found the towel hanging from a nail on the wall. A towel rack was something Cliff kept forgetting to buy.

Dinner was served and to the three of them it was one of the best meals they had ever eaten. It probably wouldn't have been a blue-ribbon winner, but the Kerrs were the most thankful family in Colorado. Cliff had fried canned salmon patties, instant potatoes, sliced canned beets, canned biscuits, and canned peaches for dessert.

The years of unpleasant experience had softened Moureen more than Cliff could account for. She didn't complain about the coffee cup rings on the table cloth or the way it was crooked on the table. The logs in the fire place were burning a fiery red, casting out shadows Cliff had watched many times before. This time, his many fantasies were real. The lamp globes were dingy, but Moureen didn't say a word. They put out enough light to be able to see beautiful expressions on the faces of three happy people.

The radio announcers were giving reports of the weather. The snow was getting deeper with the wind blowing at high speed and causing drifts of twenty feet or more in some places. Stranded airplanes left people waiting for a weather change. Cliff was glad James had time to get home before the snow got too deep. After all, it seemed so good to be snowbound with Moureen and Cliff Jr. there. It was getting time to turn in and Moureen and Cliff Jr. were very tired. Cliff got out the inflated mattress for Cliff Jr. After the sheets and blankets were put on, Cliff Jr. cuddled up in the bed. Cliff kept the fire burning all night so Cliff Jr. would stay warm. Cliff and Moureen had always preferred a cool bedroom with the door closed. Morning soon came and three happy people were up and ready for breakfast.

The radio reports on the weather were sounding much better. The snow was moving north and temperatures were rising so the snow would soon melt. By noon the airports were clear and the planes started moving again.

Betty had slept very little through the night. Sitting in a seat in a Denver airport was nothing to feel good about. Her mind wandered from Hartford, Connecticut to Lafayette, Colorado. She missed two flights because of weather conditions. She wondered now if she would be able to catch the bus out to Lafayette. A message came over a loud speaker saying, "Anyone catching a Northwestern Bus to Lafayette must be ready in ten minutes." Betty had her bags and was ready to board the bus in five minutes flat. As the bus driver opened the door, Betty was first to give him her ticket. Others were waiting their turn to get aboard. Everyone seemed to be heading for Deer Lodge. Everyone was talking about skiing conditions, saying the weather was great there. They were all getting anxious to try their skiing skills. Making the 50 icy miles seemed to take forever. At last a sign could be seen saying five miles to Lafayette.

Betty didn't realize she wouldn't exactly be in Deer Lodge when she got into Lafayette. Doing the same thing Cliff Jr. and Moureen did, Betty and Pauline (a girl Betty met on the plane going to Deer Lodge) got off the bus and walked into the Long Horn restaurant. They found a seat and waited for service. Cindy came around acting important as usual. Chewing gum, she asked, "Are you ladies from out of town? Bet you're going to Deer Lodge to ski. Yeah, you both look like skiers to me, right?" Betty and Pauline answered all her questions once with a yes. Cindy wanted more than "Yes" for answers, so she continued, "You know what? I had a lady and her son come in here yesterday. . . yeah I'm purty sure it was yesterday. They were from Boston, big shots I assume. She was dressed purty nifty. You know what? After I told her about two men coming in here from Pheasant Drive, now Pheasant Drive is left of Deer Lodge, you know. You see I know all these parts around here real well. After I told her their names were Cliff and James, she got so interested that she spilled her coffee and almost choked on her pie."

When Betty heard the long speech from Cindy the waitress, her face lit up like a Christmas tree. Betty asked Cindy, "Did I hear you right? Did you say his name was James Runyon?" Cindy smacked her chewing gum even louder and said, "The name sounds familiar." Betty asked directions for the way out there. Cindy popped her gum and said, "Ain't but one way to go. Tell you what. Call Gerald, the cab driver. He knows because he went out there yesterday. He came back bragging about the big tip the Boston woman gave him. He said that he didn't have to take her all the way to the last cabin because James Runyon gave the lady and her son a ride up there in his jeep. Boy! Did Gerald blow off about the big tip she gave him. I teased him and told him he ought to take me to see a movie. Well, he said that he had other things to do. Made me feel kind of mad. Oh! By the way, would you ladies like some coffee?"

Betty said, "Yes, please, and we would like a menu. We're both starved, and we're in a hurry."

Cindy must have called Gerald, for he walked in just as they were finishing their meal. Betty and Pauline told each other good-bye, because Betty was taking a cab and Pauline had to wait for the next ski bus. Gerald talked only when Betty forced him to. She asked about the climate and tried to act interested in skiing even though she knew nothing about it. The trip seemed endless. The roads were slick and dangerous, but that didn't seem to faze Gerald at all. Coming to a sliding stop, he asked, "Where did you say you were going?" Betty stammered and said, "I'm looking for James Runyon. Would you by any chance know where I might find him? I was told he lived on Pheasant Drive."

"Well Ma'am," said Gerald, "Pheasant Drive turns left here. It's a rough road and there's two cabins on it." Betty's heart almost touched her tongue. "I want to go on," she said. The treacherous road went on and on. Finally, Gerald said, "Now over yonder in the cleared spot is a cabin, and there's one more cabin up this road. Here's where I brought a woman yesterday. The man that lives here said that he'd take her to the next cabin. He said my car wouldn't make it up there. Do you want to stop here?" "Yes," said Betty. When Gerald stopped Betty asked him to wait and let her check before he left. She went to the door and knocked with a trembling hand. She waited for an answer then knocked again. No one answered. She knocked a third time, but there was no one there. 'Must I give up and go back to Connecticut?' she wondered.

Gerald was getting anxious to get paid and head out. He tapped his horn and said, "Snap it up. I don't have all day." Betty was beginning to get anxious and wonder what was next. "I can't go back until I find him," she thought. "He has to be here somewhere." Listening, she heard someone chopping wood. She called to the driver and told him if he'd wait a few more minutes she'd give him a tip. He nodded and leaned back in the car.

Betty started walking to the sound of the chopping, and she knew that since it wasn't far from the house, it had to be James. The closer she got to the sound of the axe the faster she walked. The wind was cold and cutting, and her lungs were hurting from the exposure. Finally she got a glimpse of a man. Before she realized what she was saying, she called out, "James Runyon." The chopping stopped. James looked around and asked, "May I help you? Are you lost?" By then she was close enough to him that he recognized her. "Betty! Is this really Betty Blake?" "Yes, James, I am Betty." By then they were in each others' arms.

James left the axe stuck in the limb he was chopping off. Words were unspoken, but the looks they gave each other were clear evidence that the spark that had almost burned out had finally been rekindled. Returning to the cabin, Betty got her bags from the taxi, payed the driver a large amount of money, and thanked him. She turned around to James and the driver drove away.

Betty set her bags down in the clean cabin, then asked James of she could stay there for a while. James being the gentleman assured her it would be OK, saying the couch wasn't very comfortable but he would sleep on it and she could have his bed in the other room. He cooked supper, but they were too excited to eat very much. It was late that night before they got caught up on all the stories that had happened since their breakup, so many years ago.

Betty woke up early the next morning to the smoke from the wood fire seeping through the cracks in the door and the smell of sausage frying. It made the day come alive. It was a new life, the beginning of happy tomorrows, for last night before they went to bed, they had put all the many things that had separated them for all these years under the rug of forgiveness. Today was a dream that had been fulfilled. After dressing in jeans and a blue jersey, Betty opened the door and stood watching James busily preparing breakfast. Feeling her presence, he looked around and saw her as she used to look, except for a few extra pounds and some wrinkles. James placed the fork he was using to turn the sausage on a table and then took her in his arms and held her firmly until the smell of burned sausage forced him to release her. The breakfast of baked canned biscuits, sausage, coffee, and a jar of strawberry preserves was soon served. This was the best breakfast they had tasted in years

Plans were already underway for a wedding. James went in to town and called his brother Fred, telling him all the latest news. "You know, Fred, when I left you some time ago you promised to come and see me. I'm holding to you–I want you to be the best man at Betty's and my wedding." Fred promised he would come if possible. James told him he'd be expecting Paula and Mary Ann too. Little did Fred know that the wedding would be in his two-room cabin in Pheasant Drive.

Cliff, Moureen and Cliff Jr. were enjoying the "Cabin in the Sky," as it had been named, but all good things must come to a close. It was time Cliff Jr. was back in school. What would the decision be? Would Moureen go back to Boston with Cliff Jr., or send him to live with a friend for the rest of the year? It was too good to be with Daddy again, and Cliff Jr. didn't want to leave: he thought they might be separated again. All of a sudden an idea came to Cliff Jr. He said, "If Daddy and James could have the road graded and gravel put on it, then Daddy could take me to meet a school bus." To Cliff the idea seemed logical.

Moureen was thinking what was best for her business back East. She knew in her heart she would never leave Cliff again. She was considering turning the business over to Lenora to run, since she was business-minded and honest. Yet there was Cliff Jr. She hated for him to have to change schools, for he was in a high-rated school. While she was busy tidying up the house, she was also trying to solve these problems. Cliff didn't offer advice, for he had never had the opportunity before. Moureen had changed since her parents had messed up her marriage. Now they were gone, and life was quite different for her now. She wanted Cliff's advice, but all Cliff wanted was a happy home with Moureen and Cliff Jr. helping make it that way.

Cliff heard James coming up the road, and he called Moureen and told her James was coming. Little did Cliff know there were two in the jeep. When James stopped in the yard, Cliff saw the second person. Cliff told Moureen there was someone with James. The door of the jeep opened and James got out and walked around to the other door, opened it, and helped a nice-looking lady out. Cliff was elated when he saw this woman–could it be Betty or was it an illusion? Moureen rushed in the bedroom and rearranged her hair, which seemed to want to droop, added lipstick, and made her way to the door. Soon James and Betty were inside the house. James' eyes were beaming like 100-watt light bulbs. James introduced Cliff to Betty, and Cliff knew then that James was experiencing the same joy he had recently experienced. Cliff had the enjoyment of introducing his wife to Betty. The women hit it off beautifully while Cliff and James were busy talking about the wild life and how many mountain goats they had seen lately.

James and Cliff left early the next morning to see about getting the road graded and gravel put on it, agreeing that Cliff pay for the two extra miles beyond James' house. Moureen was much in agreement, and Cliff Jr. was overjoyed, for he could see being transported back and forth to school. He would not have to think of having to go back to school in Boston and leaving his father.

Moureen began asking for Cliff's advice about her business. She was so completely changed from the person she had been that he was willing now to give advice which Moureen accepted. As Cliff drove Moureen to the airport in Denver, he dreaded for her to be away while she was getting her business into someone else's hands. She met Walter at a restaurant and she told him of how Cliff had accepted her and how happy she and Cliff and Cliff Jr. were. She asked Walter for the big favor of checking on her house and seeing that the tenants took care of it. She told him she had put her business in good hands. After eating, Walter went with Moureen to arrange for a moving company to load the things she owned. She wanted to get a bed so Cliff Jr. wouldn't have to sleep on the mattress. She bought a color TV, hoping someday they might be able to get electricity. She picked up Cliff's grades and was ready to head west. She barely had time to catch the plane. Walter drove her to the airport and told her he was so proud for her. Through the years he had watched her and knew her heart was pining for someone, and he always hoped it was for Cliff. She thanked him for what he had done for her in the past, but most of all for the last words he had said. Then she told him how much she loved Cliff and hoped to make it up to him in the future. Everyone boarded the plane and it took off.

Moureen came by bus from Denver to Lafayette and Cliff was there to pick her up. They arranged with the storage owners to store the furniture when it arrived. Cliff insisted they go to the Long Horn and eat. Cindy waited on their table, but she was very quiet. She must have forgotten her bubble gum for she wasn't chewing. She took their order and served them without asking one question. Maybe she didn't see any loneliness in Cliff's expressions. Anyway, he and Moreen ate and enjoyed the meal.

After eating, Cliff and Moureen went shopping for a few things. When they left for home, Cliff never told Moureen that the roads had been graded and graveled, and, another surprise, a load of lumber and other supplies had been delivered. Carpenters were coming the next day to add on a bedroom for Cliff and a living room, plus closets and cabinets for the kitchen. Moureen loved the idea. "Cliff," she asked, "if they get the rooms built in time, why don't we have the reception for James and Betty's wedding?" Cliff agreed but said it would depend on the Colorado weather and how fast the carpenters could work. They were needing work and were willing to put in long hours. They had the cabinets made in a shop outside Lafayette.

The wedding day was getting closer and closer, and Moureen and Betty were getting more anxious by the hour. While Moureen was making big plans for the reception, Betty was planning for the wedding. So many details to be taken care of. She and James had made arrangements with a violinist from back home in Connecticut to come and play for the wedding. They had contacted a Lutheran preacher to perform the ceremony, since he was pastor in a church in Lafayette and they were making plans to go there to church. He told them he would be happy to perform the ceremony.

Cliff Jr. was attending school in Lafayette. Cliff made the twice-a-day drive to take Cliff Jr. to catch a bus. The school system was different from the one in Boston. It took a bit of adjusting to get used to the change, but Cliff Jr. was willing to accept it.

The rooms were finished, and Cliff and Moureen drove to town for the stored furniture. Cliff and Moureen were busy getting things put where they wanted. The cabin took on a woman's touch. Cliff had a covered walkway, with heavy wire enclosing it, to the outside toilet. It would be safe to use since bears and other animals were close neighbors. I should say the bears were the only neighbors they didn't like being around. Cliff Jr. was enjoying his new bedroom. Cliff bought a kerosene lamp for Cliff Jr.'s room, maybe to make it seem more like it was electric. The mattress was put in a closet for use in case of an emergency.

Only three days until the wedding–a wedding which should have been years ago, but sometimes fate plays a role and things come out differently. Betty and James were busy. They were painting walls, buying furniture, and having windows put in, plus getting their wedding clothes in order and checking with invited relatives and friends. Jarred Connor, the violinist, was to be in Lafayette tomorrow. James made reservations in the Western Starlight motel for Jarred, James' brother Fred, his wife Paula and daughter Mary Ann and for a cousin, also from Hartford, and some old school friends of Betty's from Montpelier, Vermont.

The weather was being very cooperative with plenty of sunshine and just enough clouds to make the vast spaces of Colorado look peaceful and friendly to all who would come to the Blake and Runyon wedding. Betty woke up early, rubbing her hands and realizing today was the day she would change her name forever. She thought over the things that had made life miserable for them. After dressing and having coffee, Moureen went into town and rented a motel room, so they could all have a decent bath and the ladies could go to the beauty shop.

The men went from the motel to the barber shop for hair cuts and then by the cleaners for their suits. Betty went to the florist and picked up flowers. James stopped by the motel to see if everyone was there and gave directions on how to get out to Pheasant Drive. He had already made arrangements for a man with a nice van to pick the guests up and bring them out. He didn't much prefer Gerald bringing them out. The van was new and big enough to accommodate everyone. The preacher had been contacted, and he drove his own car since he knew where they lived. Betty hung up balloons at the entrance to the driveway, hoping the animals wouldn't find them and destroy them.

Moureen was very busy getting things in order for the reception. The cake had been picked up at the bakery, champagne was in the refrigerator, the punch was made, and the finger food was ready. Moureen was pleased with the addition to the house. She was especially proud of the kitchen sink. If only they had electricity, but that would have to wait. She was thinking only of one day at a time Three o'clock was drawing near. Moureen and Cliff were dressed and ready. Moureen was in a pale pink dress with matching shoes. Cliff wore a navy suit. They complimented each other on how nice they looked, as it had been so long since they had seen each other dressed up. Each one thought the other one looked better than they had ever seen them before.

The guests had arrived when Cliff and Moureen got there. Three minutes later the violinist played, "Oh, Promise Me," followed by "Ave Maria." As he started the "Bridal Chorus," and Betty was in the room on the arm of Bill, a schoolmate from Montpelier, an unusual thing happened. A herd of deer came by, stopped at the cabin, formed a circle, and many put their heads against the windows, as if they were rejoicing with the bride and groom. A covey of pheasants sat on the roof and gave out their calls. As the music stopped the pheasants went on their way and the deer turned at once and went off in pairs.

The preacher had an impressive ceremony; the bride looked brilliant in her white dress. James was handsome in his dark suit and boutonniere. Fred was James' best man. Moureen, with Cliff and Cliff Jr. did a marvelous job entertaining the wedding guests. The refreshments were great, and the friendliness shown by the host and hostess was something to add to a perfect day to be remembered by all. The van was waiting to take the guests back to Lafayette. There were hugs and kisses and tears as the guests departed. It had been a beautiful day for everyone, and to make it seem more like a fairy tale to those who read this, the weather was ideal. What more could one ask for?

A few years later, James and Betty had added rooms to their house. Electricity had been added to James and Cliff's houses, and bathrooms put in. Not only had all these things been added, but James and Betty were proud parents of three children: Frances, Elizabeth, and Jimmie. Their houses looked different. They had built around their cabins, to preserve them, holding on to the memories they had stacked inside them. Uncle Clay had died, leaving the rest of his fortune to Cliff. Moureen had sold her house and business in Boston. Cliff Jr. was through high school and trying to make up his mind where to go to college. He wanted one close enough where he could come home often for he still had the fear of losing his daddy again.

Cliff and James had changed so much since they were with their wives. Plus, their long-time friendship was even stronger. Time is such a healer. It blocks out grief and does wonders for the soul.

So long!

See ya!

MINNIE WRITES TO DAISY

Dear Daisy and all,

We aint heerd frum youns in so long, thought I'd rite and let ye no we're all a doin purty good. My ole man Mel, he had a little truble wiht he piles, but he went to the store whur thay keep medisine, and told the man that was a worken in there, what wuz rong with him, and he sole him a tube of stuff called preparation H and he used it like the man said, and he got better real quik.

I thot maybe Mel's turble cum from us a takin a big trip. I'm shore sum body tole you about me and Mel a takin a ride ona areplain. Ever body noes hit I thank. Ever body in Goose Creek does and you no how thangs is spred arounb.

Well let me tell ye about the trip. Our oldest kid, Jolene, she maried Corris Crump seval year back, and there youngen was born six months after they maried, of corse hit was pre-mature, she jest wayed nine pounds. Any way they have five more youngens, all reel purty, and all reel smart at schule, they make good grades and I tole Mel they is all the spittin imige uf me. He looked kindly disapproved, cause he was gealous and wonted them to be like him, I was jest a kiddin him o'course.

Will, I must git back on our trip. Jolene and her man Carris lives a way off in East Tennessee. Corris went up their frum whur we live hear in Goose Creek Nevada, and bought sum land, and he started raisin som king of green weeds, and now they are as rich as cream from a jersey cow. Thye dont wont enybody knowing about it fer Corris said ever body wood be a raisin hit and the price wood go down. Me and Mel thought hit sounded kinley strange. But dont let it leak out fur Corris might heer I tole yo and he wouldn't like hit a tall.

Well I'm a goin to get back at tellen ye agin. They sent us 2 round trip Areplain receipts to come to Gooberville Tennessee. I tole Mel I wuzent agoin to git offen the ground, unless I wuz hung by the neck. Mel started soft talkin me to go. I cood sea he quz jest a bustin to go see his fambily and go th that there big weddin; ones ob Jolene's gurls wuz gittin hitched. Sos I started a makin plans. I'd heerd women talkin in time, hows they got new dresses and awl two go to em. It had tuck ever thang we had made all winter offen or aigs and butter money to live on, and I didn't have eny thang to bye a knew outfit wiht.

Well, Grand Paw Ward lef all of us grand kids a little money he had worked hard for, and he tole us to keep it, until we neaded hit real good. Sose I nowed rite now I neaded it worser than I had ever neaded hit. I had it hid away in a rusty Calumet Baking Powder can, in the cellar under are livin room. We always keep our sweet taters in there, sose they want wrot, cause hit stays warm in there in winter. Anyway I got my money out, hit had bin in their so long, it had got all musty and rankled.

That saim day I got the warsh tub in, and het some water in the tea kittle, and tuck me a bath, for I had heerd people say, tha the mershants didn't wont you two tri on clothes if you smelt sweaty. I don't no what that mattered. I even washed my feet, and I had jest warshed thyem two weeks before. Anyweigh I went to Goose Creek and shopped. I tried on this purty hot pink silky like dress, it had ruffles, and purty lace and tucks all over it. I knowd as soon as I seen hit I was agoin to bye it. I said, "I want it."

Hit was kindly big on me, sis I bought a blu ribbon to ware around my waste. Then the woman said, real polite like, May I show you some shoes. I no she wuz a wonten two cell me a pare, she said, You'll need knew shoes to go wiht your knew dres. Sos I spotted a pare of purple ones, and I said thar they is. I wanted to talk polite and said these purple ones. She looked kindly puzzled but found my size. Oh Daisy! That kindly looked us over good and well.

That night thay said thay knowed we wuz tard and evethang and that we could jest stay at home and knot have to dress and go thet ther re-hearsol stuff, you go to, the night afore the big blow off. I thought I loked all write with what I wore on the plain. But my hart was stil tutchin my tonge, and I knowed it kneaded to git back in place afore the wedding, so me and Mel jest staid their and wondered around in there big house. They even have rest rooms in there house like on the plain. Ceptin theres mutch bigger and purtier. Well we finely went to bed in one uv them purty rooms whur everthang maches, and their wuz a rest room write offen the rume we slept in. HIt sure beat fittin a lantern and goin out side. Boy, I wisht we had one at home. We shore slept good on them springs in them bed ticks. We wuz all wrested the nex mornin, the day of the big weddin.

Everybody was a buzzin around, and nuthin would do Joline but fer me to take a shower inside that tub. I tole Joline I washed off afore I went to buy my new dress. But she wouldn't take no fur an anser. Well, so I got in that tub, and when that water started a poring all over me, I was skeered to death. I thought a hurricane had hit the house and tore the ruf offen it. Jolene fineally calmed me down, and she washed my hair, and dried it with a heater she held in her hands. I felt so refreshed. And I didn't even have a B.O. as her kids call it. Then I put on my purty hot pank dress, my panty hose, purple shoes, then I put on my purty green hat on, and got my red pocket book. Mel whistled til everybidy in the house heerd him. But you should a seen my Mel. He looked like a lawyer in his deseased unkles suit. Corris said he must wear a tie, sose he got him one and I tell you, he was the mostes handssomest man I have ever seed. His suit was purty tite. I was skeered it would bust open. I tole Mel agin, don't ye even belch, or you'll be in truble shore enuff. I was so exited tellin ye everythang I plum for got to tell you who wuz a gettin wed. It was Bessie, Jolene's oldest girl, that I tole about bein premature and jest wayed 9 pounds.

Well we went to the weddin, road in that big ol Catillac. When they got redy fer me two gone in, one of them men dressed in black and had a cote on with a long tale to it. (Mels looked lots better, cause hisn didn't have a tail). Anyway he looked curius at me, and helt out his arm, and I didn't no whut he meant. Mel nodded and said Minnie go ahead and walk with him. I started up that there long hall, and I keep lookin back to see if Mel is comin, and ever body in that church was a wallen there eyes and a lookin at me, and sum uv em sayen somethun to others. I thank they's jest gelus uv me and Mel. Cuz I was dressed so purty and Mel wuz so cute and all, and due you no, I wuz the only wun thare that had a hat on. Well, hit warn't long til Bessie come down that hall. She was so purty in her long white dress, but I rekon her petticoat must uv come luce, cause hit drug way behind her. I never mencined hit to her after the weddin, cause I knowed she'd blush. She caryed a bunch uv flours, as she cum down the hall, and I whispured to Joline and ast her, what wuz the flours fer, and she sed, that wuz jest to make the weddin purty. And her dress wuz all trum in shiney glittery stuff it shore wuz purty.

Her man's name is Martin Neas. He shore was dressed up and seemed to be smart. He even kissed her after the preacher preached to them and tole what all they must do. Then after that we all went to a big room, and everbody was a talkin, and Bessie and Martin wuz a posin fur picters. And finally they got thru and went to the bigust kake I ever seen, and cut sum uv it and crammed hit in each others mouth. Joline said that was tradytional. I didn't no what that word ment, but I didn't aisk. Well I'm goin to hush about that big blow off.

Well I art to close and go clean out the hen house. Maybe the hens will start layin and I can git some of the money put back in the jar Grandpa give me. I shore hope Joline and Corris can keep on raisin them there tall weeds sose Joline want ever have to git out and raise chickins and milk cows like we have to do. But I wont to remind ye agin, don't dare cheep hit about them a raisin that stuff, fer Corris shore wood be mad at me, and I wont to keep piece in the fambily.

Now I'm goin to close now fur shore, and we're goin to be a lookin fur youns all to come and stay all nite with us, and we can jest keep a tellin youns about our trip to Gooberville, Tennessee, and about the weddin. And I shore wont to show you my pretty pank dress and thangs.

Now do come soon.
Yours truly, Your good friend,
Minnie

So long!

See ya!

DAISY BLASTS MINNIE

Dear Minnie,

I'll take time to try an ancer your most interestin lettre. It shore soundid like youns' had a good time at yore doter's houce. It's shore gud to taik big trips an all, but fur me, I'de druther hold on to mi monie. Yore Grandpaw, pore thang, wood tarn over in his coffin, ifn he'd know you'd blo all his monie on sich fine close, you sed you bot. Of coarse that's yore busness, and I aint agoin to tell you what to do. But as I say, I shore cudn't a spint my pore old Gran Paw's monie like at.

I must tell ye what I've been a doin, I'm a goin to a schule. It's fer older peeple to git ejucated. I shore am a larnin a lot. How to talk polite, and howe to spel good, She's a larnin' us how to ack around peeple. One thang she said, never go along lookin back, said "that weren't polite." It maid me thank uv you, when you sed you wuz lookin bak to sea ifn yore man Mel wuz a comin' when you went up the long hall in the church fer yore granddotters weddin. I don't want ye to thank I'm trieing to lern ye whut thee teecher learnt us. But sense ye aint in schule, I thoght ye mite like fer me to tel ye how to cak, sose the nex time ye go to a weddin you want be a lookin back.

Scents I've bin a goin to schule, I feal reel proud uv myself. I can talk so propur, and my spelin is emprovised so mutch. I shure wisht you cood go to schule and git poliet. So ifn you ever go to Corris' agin you'll no moor how to ack, and talk and everthang.

I've been a thankin' of yore douter Jolene who had a baby that wayed nine pounds, and it ws a six munth old baby. I don't mean to bee a rubbin it in, but sense I'be been a goin to schule and got ejucated, I can figger thangs out. Or you shure it wuzn't a nine month old ungin? And you just cuvered thangs up. Dont git me rong, I dont mean to hurt yore feelins or nuthin, but I couldn't keap frum wonderin.

I'll tell ye abot mi grand douter, she maried Sherman Kilgore. Thay jest went to the Justus of Piece, and he maried them there in his ofus. She didn't spen a hole lot of monie on fian close. She sed she knowed she'd nead to keap it to help bye furnater and maby baby close in ten or leven monts. Thay shore didn't have to git maried. Her husband is reel nice (I lernt that word husband at schule). My teecher sed to saye husban instead of my man. I'm not trying to rub it in. I'm jest tryin to lern you, what the teecher lernt me.. I 'm a tellin ye, hit is good to have a ejucation.

I'd shore like to sea yore out fit, coarse I don't keer fur hot pink (my teecher sed two knot say pank). I thot uv you whin she sed it. Now dont thank I'm a rubbin it in. I'm jest a tryin to help ye git ejucated. And sumpthin else I don't belief I'd a bought purple shoos. Whit wuns wood a bin purty, and fer the hat yoo art to a bought a pink un. But you sed thay didn't have a big seluctin to chouse frum. I arten't to a sed all that, but I knowed you didn't no, no better, and sense I do, I jest had to help you.

I must go back to air grand dotter Bonnie June, they's gittin along reel well, her and Sherman is both reel romantic. Sherman, he's got a reel good job down at the Crows Nest saw mill. Sherman, he's the off bearer, and works long airs. Thay pay him good, he makes $3.75 a air. Bonnie June, she jest stayes at home, and hopes to hit in the famlily way reel sune. They've all reddy bin marid long enuf that peeple can't say they had to git marid. Now remimber I'm not rubbin Joline in a tole.

I bet you and Mel relly enjoyed you're visit with Corris and Joline. Youn's live so fer away and ever thing. If I wuz you I'd jest tel Corris and Joline to send you and Mel plain tickets reel offen. If thay're so rich and all. That is if thay're stayin in with the law, with them a sellin that green wead stuff. I no what that stuf is, but I'm not a cheapin it two a sole, fur you're my frind, and I want ever tel it. That is unles you'd git high and mity. I mite tel it to get even. But I dont thank you'd ever come to that, and I'm two good a Christian to ever let it hit out. I promis. Sinse I got my ejucation, I've learnt it ain't polite to corect peeple, and say hard thangs aboute them.

Well, I cood go on fer airs tellin about my schulin. But that woodn't impresh you iny, so I'll jest tel you how mutch I enjoid yore letter, and I knewed by the way you rote that that wuz a very enjoyous trip. Sure hoap you can reed this hear letter and can pronounch the big words I'm a learnin' to uze. I shure woodn't exchange my ejucation fer airy areplane trip to Tennessee. Did you git to sea eny Hillbillies when you was at Tennessee? Thay sae Tennessee is loaded with em. Bee shore and tel me, when you ancer this letter how they look. I've heerd some peeple saye that some uv em had one lag longer than the other. And do thay look like goats? Be shure and tel me ifn' thay have ejucation. I heer thay talk reel "back woodsy." I shure hope thay can go to schule, and larn to write and say poliet words like I do.

You was a talkin about Bessies peticote a hangin out behind her weddin dres, a draggin behind her. Well I learnt at schule, what it wuz, it is caled a train. My techer had picters uv her douter, when she got maried. I didn't ast her what that wuz a draggin behind her. She jest up and sed that wuz a train I didn't say mutch. I jest observed, but I wuz a thankin when she mentuned a train, that trains runs on tracks, and not on the back of a brides dres. I don't meen to try two corect ye, but I wonted to let yu no what a long peace uv cloth that's a dragginfrum a brides dres is caled. So tri two remembre its caled a train.

Minnie we wont you and Mel, and the kids to load up and cum two sea us reel sune. We'll talk all night and into Sunday. I'll tell you all about my new ejucation, how to talk polite, and maby learn you how to spell. And I'm reel anxius to sea youre knew close expectially your purty dres. I can jest sea Mel's gleam in his eyes when he seen ye so purtied up. No wunder he whisled at ye. My husban Carl had me to read yore leater to him five times. He shure did enjoy it. Heerin a bout your areplain trip, and how you admitted a bein scared and all. One thang he had me to read it so mutch, wuz; because I can reed so good now. I can put so mutch exprezion to my reedin now It souns so intertainin to heer me come over those big words.

I must close now fer shore, and go take my Grand-son's (in law) lunch to him. Shermans job is so importent he cant leave the Saw Mill to come and eat.

I'm afread he's havin to work two hard. Sherman's jest 6 foot and 13 inshes tall, and ways 395 pounds. I'm scart he wont bee phisicul abel to hold the job. Well I promised I'd clouse, and I'm a goin two. Take Cair, and don' take two meny flyen trips. Come to sea us reel sune.

Sincerely,
Daisy and Carl

P.S. stands for post script. I knowed you didnt no what it meant. The teecher said, dont say yours truly, when you rite a frindly letter. Hope you dont git hurt at what I've sed. If I've defended you in airy way please excuse me, fer you are my favrite frind. Come to sea us reel soon.

So long!

See ya!

GRANDPA

Mr. Trammel talked to Grandpa on the telephone and told him his bowels were running off. Grandpa can't hear that well and understood him to say his boars were running off. Grandpa hung up really quickly, grabbed his coat, and jumped on his horse, galloping up the road to help Mr. Trammel round up his hogs.

When he got there, Mr. Trammel was in his rocker on the front porch looking pale and sick. Grandpa told him he had come to help him get his boars in the lot. Mr. Trammel said, "Who in the world told you my hogs were out?" Grandpa said, "You did." An all out argument started just as usual when they were together. Mr. Trammel was arguing he didn't tell him and Grandpa was arguing he did. After a hot dispute between the two of them, Mr. Trammel finally thought of what he had said. Grandpa apologized for misunderstanding that Mr. Trammel had said his bowels were running off instead of his boar hogs were running off. Mr. Trammel rushed to the privy for the tenth time while Grandpa straddled his horse, Old Ben, and returned home, feeling just a bit embarrassed.

Grandma, looking up the road for Grandpa, was standing in the door letting all the flies in. She had a premonition that Grandpa would run too fast while herding the boars up and have a heart attack and maybe even die. Her imagination ran far enough that she tried to decide which one of her new dresses she should wear to his funeral. There was the black one with the lace collar, or should she wear the green and orchid flowered one?

Cassie (Grandma) was a very prissy old lady in her middle seventies, but never would she own up to being old. That just wasn't Grandma's bag. She was bright and cheerful with a bit of Irish temper. When Grandpa came in the house, Cassie was already over her mourning for Grandpa's unexpected departure from the premonition which had proven wrong for the hundredth time, and she started complaining to him about so many flies he had let in by holding the door open. Cassie wasn't as mentally alert as she was at sweet sixteen. Grandpa could get a little huffy too at times, and he raised the roof a little and denied holding the door open. All of a sudden Cassie's mind cleared up and she realized it was she who had held the door open while she was grieving over Grandpa's death, which hadn't happened.

Being so pleased of his escape from sudden death, her passion overpowered her and she fell into Grandpa's arms and for a while they relived their courtship, which was near 50 years ago. Grandpa smudged Cassie with many, many amber kisses. After all, you never get too old to love, or to help your neighbor round up his prize boar hogs.

So long!

See ya!

GREAT GRANDFATHER FERDINAND

Ferdie called his great-grandfather and asked him for a big favor. Being the old fellow's namesake made him the favorite grandson. Ferdie, as he was called by his family and friends, was named for his great-grandfather Ferdinand Quincy DeRosser, whose parents had come to America from Italy. Ferdie was around 25 years old, and he was anything but handsome or smart. He wore a mustache, and his blonde hair was pulled back and tied with a gold ribbon. Scars on his face were evidence of many fights he had experienced in younger years. His squeaky voice somehow made you think he was a real sissy. But, being Ferdinand's pick of the crop, he usually got whatever he asked for.

Ferdie would call his great-grandfather and ask how he was feeling and if he had been playing golf, finally getting to the main thing he was calling for. He hemmed and hawed around for awhile, dropped the telephone with a bang twice, and then popped the question: "Grandfather, I hate to ask you for such a big favor, but if you'll loan me $4,000 to get started on, I will take a course in law enforcement. I think I could become an FBI agent and maybe be able to go overseas and help to control the drugs that are being imported to America." Grandfather Ferdinand wasn't too impressed with the idea, but because it was Ferdie he agreed and promised to have a check in the evening mail. Because Ferdie had called collect, great-grandfather quickly told him he loved him and hung up.

Ferdie waited and watched for Santa Claus. The check came on time and Ferdie rushed out to see about taking the course. He had to take an entrance test, and like all other tests he had ever taken, he flunked it sure and certain. He couldn't face great-grandfather, so he just decided to buy a ticket to some far-away place. Maybe to Italy; he had always wanted to see the "Leaning Tower of Pisa," which he thought would be educational. He also wanted to see all the other places of interest in other towns, such as Milan, Genoa, Florence, and especially Venice, where he could see the cathedral of Saint Mark. Then when he returned he could tell the great-grandfather all about it and maybe not get scolded for spending the school money he had borrowed. "Or would he even listen when I tell him the stories I'll have to tell?" Fergie wondered. 'I'll tell him all about the patron saint of Venice, after whom the cathedral was named, plus the beauty, location, artistic destinations and literary associations. Now great-grandfather really will be proud of me. Then when I tell more about Venice, he'll think I'm really becoming classy. I'll explain how Venice lies on a cluster of small mud islands at the head of the Adriatic Sea (he won't know that either). Just wait until I tell him that Venice has canals for streets, and you ride in gondolas for taxicabs. His eyes will get big when I tell him all about the huge palaces along the banks of the Adriatic.'

'Then I'll tell him Rome is the capital and largest city of Italy. I've never been too informed on anything, so he'll think I have found some real good brain pills and be envious, just wait and see. Chances are I just might get so involved in all the romance and beauty, I might never come back. But then there's Fran; can I give her up for all these fanciful things?'

Ferdie had read ahead about Italy in a National Geographic while he was munching popcorn and sipping on a Pepsi. He wondered if he should he go ahead and experience it or go back to Fran. Wanting experience got the best of him, so he packed his bag and drove to the airport. He sauntered up to the ticket agent and purchased a ticket out of great-grandfather's hard-earned money, feeling good about the ticket that would take him to the boot-shaped country.

After the plane had circled around and around and was taking off the runway, old Ferdie's food he had eaten earlier was beginning to repeat. Ferdie became pale and his long yellow hair started rising and standing on end. The plane trip was bumpy, and Ferdie failed to relax, but they arrived on schedule. Ferdie gathered up his belongings, and, stepping off the plane, he started out to seek his fortune, just as he had for the past number of years. He had never been able to grasp the pot at the end of the rainbow, but maybe this time would be different.

The Italians soon found out Ferdie was an American, or maybe an object from outer space. It was more of a shock to him; he was staring at things, almost dazzled at all the things Italy had to offer. He was in the town of Florence, but to Ferdie it was just Italy.

After days of wandering around on the streets of Florence unable to speak their language, he became weary and even bitter that fate had played such a dreadful trick on a nice, young, handsome man like him. Every day became harder for him to endure. He couldn't get from Florence to the other towns that he had planned to experience so he could come back home and gloat about them. Finally he made up his mind to return to his home in the good old U.S.A. He was homesick for Fran.

The big nonstop Continental plane rose off the runway. Ferdie was wondering how he would find the climate back in his home town in Baltimore and how he'd find Fran. He had been away seemingly a long time. He had been away on a very special government mission, which only he and a few others know about. It had been nerveracking and tiresome, just one important meeting after another. It was relaxing to lie back in the rear of the plane, even if the weather was rough and turbulent.

The flight was treacherous, but it ended safely as the plane landed near his home town. Finding the weather typical of November's cold and snow, Ferdie grabbed his bags and headed for home. The roads were icy and Ferdie was so tired that he decided to stop off at his parents' house for the night. It was close by and he needed the rest. Mom and Pop were delighted to have him spend the night. Mom made the bedroom he had grown up in warm and comfortable. Ferdie called Fran and visited for a while and then turned in. He then reminisced of his childhood and fell into a restless sleep.

Pop came up to his room to check on him as he was making queer sounds and tumbling and tossing. Returning to bed, he told mom Ferdie was just tired and needed rest.

In the morning, as Ferdie sat at the breakfast table reading the paper and sipping coffee, he asked Mom, in a very serious way, "How did great-grandfather Ferdinand look? Did he wear a little white mustache, and have deep blue eyes, with a whimsical smile, slim and not very tall?" Mom said, "Yes, son, why do you ask?"

"Last night I had a very unusual dream. I dreamed grandfather was standing by my bed, and I asked him for a large amount of money, to go seek my fortune, and without hesitating he gave it to me. But I was a blonde, with freckles and pimple scars. Here I am a brunette! I spent time in Italy, not accomplishing anything."

Mom told Ferdie he had been his great-grandfather's choice of all the great-grandchildren. "He always said he would see that you got anything you ever wanted, if it was an education, or traveling, or, if you preferred, a hardware store, but grandfather Ferdinand didn't live to see his wishes come true. He only lived long enough to help celebrate your third birthday. You know the little train on a track in your bedroom? That was a birthday gift from him. I just couldn't ever tell you that it was his last gift he ever gave you."

She continued, "You know Ferdie, maybe he came back just for awhile; you described him just as he was. Strange things happen that we just can't understand. But, your father and I are glad you came to visit and stayed the night with us. It was just like old times." Ferdie hesitated, looked up at mom and said, "I'm glad I saw him as he was, but I'm so thankful it was only a terrible nightmare instead of reality." Looking up at the clock, Ferdie grabbed his coat, thanked them for the night's lodging, and said he must be on his way. He was anxious to see Fran; time had seemed so long.

On his way home he relived the nightmare and seeing great-grandfather; it seemed real spooky. He was glad he was a sucessful businessman. Maybe the nightmare happened because his great-grandfather wanted him to not become complacent.

Getting home and being with Fran again made him happy and contented. Someday he will tell Fran about it and hope great-grandfather got back safely to the spirit world. That's all Folks!

So long!

See ya!

ELECTION AT PANAMA CITY

The time had come for the politicians of the city to make up their minds if they would be running for an office. It just so happened that Chris Newberry finally made his decision to run for mayor in a city with a population of 3,678 people. (That was the count a week before Jim and Laura Grubbs' 9-pound and 10-ounce son was born.)

Chris was making big mental plans as to what he could do for the city to bring big industry in and have better garbage pickup and recycling; he also thought the city should pay for baby sitters for working mothers. Believing he could get a bill passed to raise old age benefits (of course, that would have to be taken to Washington, D.C.), he put that one on his platform too. He thought he must promise the citizens he would lower the electric, gas, and water bills, for everyone was complaining about them sky rocketing. He firmly believed he could cut these bills in half, or that was what he had in mind to tell the voters. The Post Office needed a brick cleaning, but, thinking it over, he decided that was government property, and he could spend the city's money for better things. Scratching his head and thinking of another big promise, he thought he could include Christmas and all the decorations (anything for another vote).

He would definitely see that a huge evergreen tree would be hauled in from maybe Oregon or Washington–bringing it in from a northern state would be even more effective–and placed on the town square. He would add new lights such as Panama City had never seen before, plus a live nativity scene, with people and animals flown in from the Far East to play the part of what had happened almost two thousand years ago. Chris thought this expense would come out of the city's budget. All senior citizens over 65 would get free transportation anywhere within the city limits (which didn't reach very far), and they would get free meals during the Christmas season. He wanted to be fair to everyone (to get their votes, of course), so he included free meals to everyone on

Christmas day. The meals would include turkey, ham, dressing, salads, gravy, vegetables, cakes, pies, puddings, eggnog and plenty of coffee. He could really see the votes adding up when he put that promise down on paper. Another idea hit him: every woman would receive a dozen long stemmed red roses on her 40th birthday. He knew the town wouldn't have to pay for too many, since most women stay 39 until they get crippled with arthritis and their hair turns gray.

There were the children, he thought to himself; don't leave them out or you'll lose the election. Every child under 14 years would get a choice of a tricycle, bicycle, Nintendos, computers, dolls, doll buggies, doll houses, doll furniture, Barbie dolls and clothes, stuffed animals, little girls' make-up sets, puzzles, games of all kinds, gloves, toboggans, candy, fruits, and a big wish for a "Merry Christmas!"

Chris was feeling good about all his plans and felt sure this was the platform that would put him in office as Mr. Mayor of Panama City in the coming election. He kept thinking if he had left out any promises. Oh yeah–he must cut the senior citizens' utility bills far below what he had already slashed and to give them armed protection at all times. He had a feeling they wouldn't remember half of his promises, but he would get their vote. He wasn't through day dreaming. He'd promise to paint every house that needed painting in the voting area, then build new sidewalks and plant trees and flowers to help make the city a paradise for tourists. He would make sure they came to see such a fast-growing city flourish under the new management of such an intelligent young man as Mr. Newberry considered himself. He thought of himself as handsome, well thought of, well groomed at all times, with sparkling teeth and smile that would entice the most beautiful girl in the United States and maybe Canada. But somehow, someway, Mr. Newberry was the only one who saw himself that way. Others saw him as he was.

Feeling good about all the promises he was about to put on paper, Chris fell back in his recliner and had a long relaxing nap. After waking up and feeling much better, he got out his old typewriter. He had made F's in high school, for he never turned in a good typewritten paper. In fact, after some of the higher officials of the city checked his school records, they found that he had barely passed by one point. Chris never expected anything like this ever happening, their checking on him as if he were a criminal. Of course the officials kept it quiet, even though they were very much against him and his platform. Chris had caught them squandering money that belonged to the city treasury.

Chris started typing away, being very careful to put in every detail of his great promises.

The election day was drawing closer and closer, and Chris was going from door to door asking the people for their votes. Many promises were made, mostly to senior citizens, for he had offered them some square deals. The poor elderly people could barely hear or comprehend the details, but they were hoping for better days and promised him their votes. Day after day Mr. Newberry went from house to house, giving out cards with his handsome (he thought) picture on it, saying "Vote for the man who can bring Panama City to its highest peak." The mayor in office didn't seem to like it very well.

After a day of hard electioneering, Chris thought he had better write down things he must do before his big speech, Saturday afternoon: First, make sure I kiss all the babies, especially the Grubb baby, tell Mrs. Grubb how pretty she is, and that the baby looks just like her. So there's one vote. Second, tell Veronica Valtese how lovely she looks in her new hat. Third, get Walter Snapp a plug of apple tobacco. Fourth, tell the girl next door to Mr. Snapp just how beautiful she is, and that she should run for Panama City's queen next year, for I'm going to promote a big celebration. I'll get the rest of my money that Uncle Cyrus gave me years ago out of the bank, and I'll quit biting my fingernails. Then I can get my suit out of the cleaners, have my car washed, polish my shoes, be sure to wear my new red, white, and blue tie so I'll look patriotic, be very sure to use Certs. I will set my clock to alarm early, be sure to eat a big breakfast, take a shower, push wave in my hair, wear socks I got from mom for Christmas. I can't stand old lady Bumgarner but I'll tell her how nice she looks in her new glasses, and be sure to ask how much they cost, for she just loves to tell the price of things (if she thinks it costs more than what others pay). I'll ask Mr. Weithers as I go by the bank how he is feeling, as if I could even care. I will take an umbrella if it's raining to hold over some mother and baby (just for another vote), practice smiling, don't forget to pause after making a big promise (to give people a chance to applaud), be sure the city hall is lined in chairs (it holds 500 people). I can ask policemen to guard me as I make my speech, bow graciously as I enter the room, take time to shake hands of people near the aisle as I march up to the podium, clear my throat, then ask the audience to be seated.

After studying the 25 things he needed to do and keep in mind, he thought everything was going well. He was thinking, "Today at 2:00 p.m. eastern daylight time I will be giving my historical speech, one that will go down in the annals of history."

To make sure everything was in readiness, Chris checked over his speech again, and, not being too sure of himself as far as memory was concerned, he thought it was best to take his well-written paper copy along. Since he was getting tense and time was getting away, Chris accidentally picked up his list of things to do instead of his speech.

He used his mouth wash, put the wave in his hair, and checked to see if his freshly cleaned suit looked presentable (it looked just fine, and he had thought to wear the new socks mom gave him for Christmas, and he had remembered his red, white and blue tie bought purposely for this occasion just to look patriotic.) He then got into his freshly washed car and sped through the town on his way to city hall, feeling fine.

As he entered the auditorium it was overflowing–but mostly for curiosity, not for what he had to tell them. Remembering to put on a candidate's smile, which would have cost only 29 cents from Wal-Mart if he could have bought it. He remembered to bow great big, walked up to the podium, and laid his well-(or not-so-well-) typed speech out on the podium. By then he was getting a little stage fright; more was coming on by the seconds. Clearing his throat and trying to say "Good afternoon to my friends and co-workers," he made only a queasy sound, turned pale, and started reading his list of things he had written out to do. He didn't realize the mistake he made, but when he got down to telling Mrs. Valtese how lovely she looked in her new hat, this sort of brought him back to his senses, for he never could stand the precise old lady. Realizing what a blunder he had made, he grabbed his paper and took out the back door.

Chris' Uncle Cyrus was so embarrassed over the event, he drew money from the bank for a one-way ticket to Wyoming, telling Chris he always thought he would make a better cowboy than a mayor. Chris was more than pleased at Uncle Cyrus's generosity. He grabbed some suit cases and packed his belongings, caught a bus and, as he left, waved good-bye to his family and friends.

He still had the wave in his hair, his patriotic tie on, and the socks mom gave him for Christmas. He may look a little odd if he wears that gaudy tie riding through buck brush and tumble weeds. But heck, the West's a big place; probably more room out there for a guy like Chris than in a town of 3,679.

Didn't hear who was elected as the new mayor–probably the same fee-grabber that was already in. Good luck Chris in your new adventure, and be careful not to fall off the house!

So long!

See ya!

MRS. DOOLEY AND HER WHITE RABBIT

A few years ago, Mrs. Dooley was a lonely old lady (even older than me) living alone after her beloved Roscoe died. Roscoe had been old enough to die many years before, but he was called at the age of . . . well, a way up there. I would tell but Mrs. Dooley might object.

The reason for his departure was his young-at-heart feelings. He was trying to accomplish something he had longed to do for many decades, and that was to learn to roller-skate. Mrs. Dooley greatly objected to the idea, but Roscoe, being stubborn and old, refused to obey Mrs. Dooley's wishes. He slammed the door as he started out, stumbling down the street to a sports store. He ordered the clerk to show him a pair of roller skates, the best they had. The clerk asked if he was buying them for a grandchild's birthday. He abruptly answered, "No, I want them for myself. Now if you'll just show me a pair with rubber wheels and air brakes, I'll pay you and be on my way home." The clerk coughed, cleared his throat and blew his nose to keep from laughing right in Roscoe's face. He explained to Mr. Roscoe that they didn't carry that kind of skates. Roscoe settled for the best kind they had, paid the clerk and left for home, feeling proud of the purchase. He was tired from his wobble back home and sat down to rest for awhile. Mrs. Dooley brought his alka-seltzer to him and in a short time old Roscoe was up and putting his skates on. Then he ventured out.

Poor Mrs. Dooley ached with a nervous pain as she saw her beloved Roscoe make his fatal plunge into destiny. He never knew what killed him. It happened on the first roll of the skates, when he fell flat on the street, hitting his head on a fire hydrant. He never gained consciousness, dying with his skates on. Mrs. Dooley was so regretful that she didn't have Roscoe eat the piece of lemon pie that Laura Greene had brought him. She did feel gratified, though, that he had taken his alka-seltzer.

Poor Roscoe was laid to rest (with his skates on) in the old family cemetery, just outside the city limits of Cottonville, Iowa. Mrs. Dooley bought a beautiful marble tombstone for his grave with an inscription that read: Dear Roscoe, you rolled out of my life in great dignity, leaving no scars to mar your identity as a great performer on roller skates. In years to come, on decoration day, someone might rub the smudge off his marker and credit him as a world champion skater. Well, so what! If it made Mrs. Dooley feel good giving him credit where credit was undeserved, then so much for Mrs. Dooley.

Mrs. Dooley believes firmly in re-incarnation, and she felt sure Roscoe would return, maybe as a young man. She even considered cutting the big ball of grey hair which she wore on the back of her head off and getting a permanent. She had never worn bright colors, but she thought of getting a pretty red dress and red shoes. She was still thinking Roscoe would soon return as a young man.

One day Mrs. Dooley had been to the grocery store for coffee, corn flakes, and a bar of Ivory soap, and as she passed by a pet shop, she saw this pretty white rabbit with beautiful pink ears. Robert (one of the clerks) had been practicing ventriloquism, and he just had to try it on Mrs. Dooley to maybe cheer her up, even though she was still coming out of mourning.

Robert heard Mrs. Dooley believed in reincarnation. As the rabbit was working his lips, Robert called out from behind a raccoon cage, "Oh dear, Mrs. Dooley, I miss you so much." All the time he was talking, the pretty white rabbit was busy working his mouth, and the voice seemed to come directly from him. In great astonishment, Mrs. Dooley yelled, "OH! My Roscoe! I knew you'd come back to me." Then Robert said again, "Please buy me, Mrs. Dooley, so we can be together again." Mrs. Dooley yanked her skirt up, unrolled her stocking and took out a big roll of bills, and told Robert she wanted the rabbit that talked. Robert assured her he hadn't heard the rabbit. Paying a huge sum of money for the rabbit, Mrs. Dooley walked out the door. Robert said one more thing: "Mrs. Dooley, call me Rossie, for I never did like the name Roscoe." Mrs. Dooley patted Rossie on the head and said, "I knew you'd come back to me."

Heading for home and now even more firmly believing in reincarnation, Mrs. Dooley made great plans for her and Rossie. When she got home she placed Rossie on Mr. Dooley's chair and handed the rabbit Mr. Dooley's pipe, but Rossie just wiggled his pretty pink ears and stared into space. She called to him to be comfortable while she put the groceries up. When she returned Rossie had disappeared. Mrs. Dooley almost became hysterical. Stirring up dust all over the house, she looked for her beloved reincarnated Rossie. Finally Rossie stuck his pink ears around the edge of Mr. Dooley's chair. "Ah, Rossie," said Mrs. Dooley, "You're such a tease, just like you were when you were a man. Of course Rossie did not know what she had said; he just twisted his nose and wriggled his ears.

When bedtime came, Mrs. Dooley turned the bed covers back and told Rossie it was bedtime. Rossie ignored her and hopped to his pan of rabbit food. Mrs. Dooley had spiced it up with cinnamon and sugar, which caused Rossie to twist his nose more than ever. Finally Mrs. Dooley caught Rossie and put him in bed with her, but who ever heard of a rabbit sleeping on a feather bead? Mrs. Dooley hadn't much more than made him comfortable when he hopped up and away he ran, hiding under the kitchen sink.

Mrs. Dooley had failed to close the cabinet door and poor Rossie knocked a lid off a molasses jar and got his pretty pink ears all gooed up with the sticky stuff. Mrs. Dooley found Rossie and scolded him severely for what he had done; Rossie only twisted his mouth and tried to wiggle his ears, but he had too much sticky on them to wiggle.

Days passed and Mrs. Dooley became very annoyed. She actually wished Rossie had not come back. He was refusing to talk, and she still missed his companionship. She often wondered why he didn't just come back as a man instead of a pesky rabbit.

One day Mrs. Dooley put a leash around Rossie's neck and let him hop down the street with her. As she came by the pet shop she stopped to see if Robert could explain why Rossie hadn't spoken a word since she took him home. The other clerks kept quiet and let Robert get out of the mess he had gotten into. Robert muttered around a little and then confessed that he had been practicing ventriloquism and thought maybe he could make her happy. Mrs. Dooley looked flabbergasted and almost fainted. After getting hold of herself, she calmly said, "I've been a ninny. Who would ever believe a rabbit could talk? As far as believing in reincarnation, people can believe if they want to."

Mrs. Dooley left the rabbit for re-sale and threw the leash in, too. As she walked home, she thought, 'Well, I know Roscoe would want me to be happy, even if it took an old gentleman to do it.' That was just what Mrs. Dooley did. She got her red dress and her red shoes and had her grey hair clipped and curled and headed down to the square dance at the senior center. There she met Earl, a sweet, quiet gentleman with no interest in roller skates. Even if you are old, it's never too late to love and be loved.

So long!

See ya!

WHICH ONE WAS BIGGER

A flu epidemic that hit Mooresville S.C. caused a large number of the women belonging to the "Music Club" to be absent from their February meeting. In fact, only six well-dressed drivers of Cadillacs, well-educated women, were able to attend. And believe me, they were well-dressed! For that was the main thing of the meeting: half of the number of women couldn't find middle C on a piano. A better name would have been, "Better Dressed Than You" Club. Anyway, Sarah, Mary, Gloria, Patricia (who was always called Pat), Frances, and Anna were the lucky ones that escaped the flu. The president, Joan, was confined to bed with a double dose of it, she was unable to attend, Faye, the treasurer was still unable to get out, and poor Alice, the vice-president, was coming down with it.

Here these six brave women had ventured out and the afternoon could not be wasted. After a few minutes of silence, Gloria said to the other women, "Did you hear about Bill Sneed and Fran Jones waiting so long to get married?"

"No," said the others.

"Well," said Gloria, "Bill is so stingy he waited six years for a sale to go on marriage licenses. Finally his mother gave him the money for the license for she was so stingy she didn't want to feed him any longer."

Sarah said, "Oh, yes, I remember that, Bill got his stinginess from his mother and his Aunt Catheryn. I heard she put all her money in a bank in Switzerland so she could get on welfare."

Mary said, "Well, that's nothing, I know of a woman in the western part of the state who complains to everyone she meets of having a splitting headache and asks for aspirins so she can supply her family with them when they get sick."

Frances, who was keeping quiet, finally said, "Discussing such stingy issues, makes me think of my neighbor's distant cousin. They used to string popcorn to decorate their Christmas tree, and after the decoration was taken down, they ate the popcorn."

Anna spoke up and said, "That's nothing. Silas Hayes turns his motor off when he starts down a steep hill to save gasoline and goes so fast he's halfway up the next hill before he has to turn his motor back on."

Pat said, "You know how Jane Jolly chews gum all the time. People say she picks it up off the street after its been chewed. I've never caught her doing it, though."

Mary said, "I think this will really cap the stack: you all know John Hall's brother Henry's ex-wife. Well, this is why Henry divorced her: she had a cavity in a jaw tooth and it was really hurting her so much, and she complained about the dentist charging so much.

So she borrowed an electric drill from Luck and Frank (her neighbors) and drilled the cavity out, then borrowed cement from them and filled the hole. She promised to pay them for the cement but she never did. This was just more than Henry could endure, and he finally divorced her and married Claudia Henry, who was divorced herself and had five children."

Frances was smiling when she told this whopper: she said Fern Holder was so stingy she made her family use toilet paper a second time.

Pat said she was ashamed to let people know that she knew Coleen Crow, but when her mother died and after her burial Coleen went back to the grave, gathered up the flowers and took them back to the florist and collected all she could from them.

Anna said Georgia Sams collected money from the Salvation Army and used to have her lips tattooed so she wouldn't have to buy lip-stick, and in the meantime it made Sarah think of Flossie Greenway, wiping rouge off her face and reusing it.

Gloria said, "You know how crazy Jean Hathway is over Fred Stiles. They say she won't let him kiss her on the lips, so her lipstick won't wear off."

Gloria said she heard her daddy say that old lady Gladys and Bob Dennis used to catch lightening bugs in summer and turn them loose in the house for light to save kerosene.

Frances said her grandfather told of a couple who used to stop their clock at night to keep it from wearing out and would get up when the roosters started crowing in the morning.

May said Vera Balch had a beautiful voice but she was so stingy she wouldn't sing, afraid she'd wear it out.

Pat told of this middle-aged woman buying a new dress who bought it four sizes too big so she would get more for her money.

Sarah spoke up and told about a woman she knew named Loretta. She left one of the T's out to save ink.

The ladies all became hoarse and agreed they had better adjourn. This goes to show us all that regardless of how well you dress or what priced car you drive or how well educated you are, we are all humans and inside us there is just a little curiosity and usually a little streak of gossip, and we all listen for it, don't we?

I'm like Joe Friday in "Dragnet" (many years ago): the names were changed to protect the innocent, meaning me. It's all fiction anyway, you knew that of course.

So long!

See ya!

COME BACK TO THE HILLS

Matthew Powers was one of the best reporters at one of the leading newspapers in New York City. He could write about an incident in a way that would interest anyone who read about it. He could put pictures into words in a way that no other reporter could ever do. Many times he would catch himself dreaming of a story he would like to paint in print. Finally, Matthew decided where he wanted to go and asked for a few days off. It wasn't easy for the best reporter to get time off for no particular reason, as it seemed to his bosses. After a while, the editor agreed that he could go, with one stipulation: he must bring back a story.

Matthew had his car serviced, packed his bags, and assured his wife and little girl that he would be gone only a few days. He knew he was heading south, but he didn't give anyone any idea of his destination. Actually he wasn't sure just where he was headed. He had always wanted to see the hills of East Tennessee and meet the friendly people he'd heard about who were blessed to live there. The further he drove, the more anxious he became, asking himself, 'Where are you going?' Matthew answered his own question aloud: "I don't know but I'm being led." Sometimes we can't see Angels, but they are there, and this one was telling him in his inner mind just where to go.

After driving for several hours, he was in Tennessee on Interstate I-40 heading west. He wondered just how far he was supposed to go. Suddenly he saw a sign that read, "5 miles to Heidelburg, Tennessee, population 5,694." He knew that was the place that he was supposed to go. Taking the exit, he found a restaurant, "Murphy Inn." He was getting hungry and a late breakfast was what he needed. After eating, he picked up a road map and saw that Heidelburg was on Highway 47, a very curvy looking road. With great astonishment he said aloud, "That's the place." Everyone in the restaurant looked at him with a suspicious look, wondering what he could be meaning. They wondered under their breath if he could he be an FBI agent, someone hunting for marijuana, or maybe just someone looking for an old friend or relative. Matthew paid for his meal and left everyone with a suspicious feeling.

After driving several miles on Highway 47, he came in sight of another road, which was marked Indian Gap. "Sounds good to me," he thought, "I'll try it." After taking the exit and driving another mile or so, he came upon another road that was unpaved and bumpy. Dust followed him like fog on an early morning. There to his left was a rusty mailbox with a name written on it in red paint: "Chris and Emily Colby," box number 85. Matthew knew then that this was where he had been led to. As he drove up the partially graveled driveway, he looked to his right and saw what he had been wanting to see for so long, the green hills and the beautiful deep blue scalloped mountains of East Tennessee. Nothing else in nature could compare with the scene he was seeing.

Driving further on he came within sight of a house that in another time might have been considered pretty, but time had taken its toll and had taken with it all that had ever been considered nice. He thought a great story might be inside this tumble-down house. Stopping his car at the edge of a freshly mown lawn, Matthew opened the car door, wondering just what to expect. He walked slowly to the door and, glancing around at what he saw, he became hesitant. "No," he thought, "I won't go back, I've been sent here, and I'm going to try." Knocking on a patched screen door, he could see inside the house and finally a woman appeared. She showed no sign of being excited at seeing a stranger. She greeted him with a "Good Morning" and asked, "May I help you?"

Matthew knew from her appearance that she was a lady. He introduced himself and told her he was a reporter from New York and he worked for The New York Times newspaper, then he asked if he might come in and interview her. Emily replied in a very friendly manner, "If my husband Chris was here, I'm sure it would be O.K., but he's afraid for me to invite strangers in when he's away, and we are so far away from anyone." Matthew assured her she would be perfectly safe, and Emily realized she would be. After inviting him in she offered him a seat on the worn-out couch with the springs cutting through the upholstery.

Glancing down on the clean linoleum rug, he saw the worn places where the wood floor could be seen.

After a few words were exchanged Emily asked if he would like a cup of coffee, and Matthew accepted very politely. While Emily was preparing the coffee, Matthew looked things over as quickly as possible. The door to a bedroom was open, and he could see a bumpy mattress on a bed, covered in a clean but worn-out spread. Everything he saw told him there had been no replacements in the house in years. He was wondering about her husband: Was he a bum? An alcoholic? Did he really care? Just then Emily came from the kitchen with a cup of coffee and a bran muffin. He didn't have to wonder if it was clean. He had already seen in her qualities that so many people lack.

After drinking the coffee with the muffin he was ready to get down answers to the questions he had come to ask. What he wanted was a story and he was ready to get it. As Emily talked, Matthew wrote it all down, hurriedly. She asked if he wanted a story from her earlier years. "Oh, yes, indeed," said Matthew. Making it as brief as she could, she told him of her parents and her one sister and two brothers. "My parents wanted us to have a good education and to be good, reliable citizens; they kept us in church and all the church activities. I was very popular, and if I might say, I used to be very attractive."

She hesitated and said, "Maybe you don't know, but some young people would give up everything for someone they love. Well, I did just that. Chris and I were both juniors in high school. We fell so deeply in love and no one could change our minds. We were determined to get married and with all the pleading our parents did we didn't change our minds. I was only seventeen and Chris was eighteen. Mom and dad gave us a nice wedding and Chris' parents gave us money for a short honeymoon. Well, the knot was tied, and it still holds firm today. We celebrated our fortieth wedding anniversary in June. In fact we only talked about it. We didn't have any way to celebrate, just no money.

"It was hard getting started out, living on our own, but that happens to all newly married couples. Chris' parents and my parents helped all they could. My father rented this house to us and the two acres of land, and that has been so helpful to us through these forty years.

"We were lucky in finding good jobs, being as young as we were. I found a job in a factory making underwear. Daddy wanted to help us all he could and sold us the house and the land. We worked hard and managed well. We bought what furniture we still have, except for replacing some appliances. Chris had a good job in a steel mill. After waiting four years we were blessed with a son, who we called Julian. Chris insisted on me quitting work to take care of the baby. I thought it was a good idea. After two years with Julian another addition came along–a son we named Mark. Chris was being advanced in his work often, and with his advancement, and our two acres of land, we were able to grow all our vegetables, and we had chickens and a cow for our milk. We didn't realize things could change and cause us so much heartache. We knew in a few years our sons would be in school, and we were putting back every penny we could save for their education. Julian was now four and Mark was two, then along came another son, whom we named Paul. All mothers would love to have a daughter, but we decided three sons would be all we could properly educate."

Emily hesitated, and asked if he would like to hear about the sons. Matthew said, "Indeed I would."

"Well," said Emily, "All moms like to brag about their children and husbands. But you know, life is like a rose bush, the blooms are so fresh and sweet smelling, and you pluck off a pretty bud, and a thorn sticks in you finger. It must be pulled out, and it leaves a place which heals in time with kind words and kisses. What I'm saying is, we've had the roses with the thorns, but you know God didn't know promise us thornless roses. We've had a wonderful life together, and I wouldn't have it any other way. As I look over the hills to the mountains, I know that some day justice will come our way. I'll tell you all about that later. First the good part.

"We were so blessed with our sons. We had three very intelligent children. School wasn't quite as easy for Paul as it was for Julian and Mark. He had to study much harder but he had the determination to stick with it, and he did. He didn't take time off from studying to be as sociable as his brothers were. Julian and Mark were ball players. Julian played football and was quarterback on the team. Mark played basketball but liked the girls better than the games and wasn't a first-class ball player. I'll never forget how handsome they all looked in their tuxedos when they went to their senior proms."

She looked into the distance as she spoke, as if she were reliving the days when her sons were still at home. "We tried to keep them dressed as nice as the other boys were dressed. We wanted them to have what we missed out on having, but as I said before we wouldn't want our marriage to have been any other way.

"Julian is our oldest son. I'll tell you about him. He was eager to learn; at an early age he was jabbering and pointing at letters when he saw them. By the time he was three, we could understand what he was saying and he was reading. He was always at the top of his class and graduated with a four-point average. He kept it up through college and made straight A's. After he got through law school and went to work, he married a nice young woman from New York, and we haven't heard from them in a long time."

Emily asked if he wanted to hear about the other sons, and Matthew told her that was what he was there for. Emily said, "I'll tell you about Mark next. He too made straight A's but he had Julian beat as far as popularity was concerned. He's better looking than Julian and always had a way of winning a girl's heart. He's very handsome, too, with brown wavy hair (like his dad's) and deep blue eyes. He is very witty and has a very friendly disposition. He's the shortest of the three at only 5 feet and 8 inches. Mark got his degree in business marketing, and after graduating he got a job in Baltimore, Maryland. The last time we heard from him he told us the business was really paying off. He too, is married, to a girl in Baltimore. You know some kids just don't, or will not, take time to write, and we can't afford a telephone.

"Here's Paul's story. He was a very hard worker and more thoughtful than Julian and Mark." Emily hesitated and seemed to be in deep thought. She finally said, "I remember when his daddy gave him his allowance, he would save it and go to the 5 and 10 cent store and buy me gifts for Mother's Day, birthdays, and Christmas. He always remembered his father on special days. Julian and Mark were never as thoughtful. Paul has always been very quiet. He played the trombone while he was in high school but gave it up after he started to college. He loved nature, and he claimed the mountains as being his. He often told me when he was growing up that when he became a man and had loads of money he would build us a new house. When I look at this one falling apart I think of what he said. Children plan great things when they are growing up but they soon forget in the hurry-scurry of a busy life. Paul got his degree in mechanical engineering. He is a co-owner in a big engineering company in Dayton, Ohio. In his last letter several years ago he told us he was getting married soon."

Emily asked again if Matthew would like more coffee. He said, "Oh, yes, and I'd love another bran muffin." After eating her muffin and drinking some coffee, Emily was ready to get back to talking. Matthew said, "Now are you ready to tell me more about you and Chris?" After seeing their house, he was anxious to hear the story.

She said, "Well, you know Chris and I have been very fortunate in raising our family. The boys were always very obedient, and didn't cause any trouble. We've been blessed with good health. But, financially it has been miserable. Sending three boys through college took so much money that we just had to borrow. It seems John Wilder is the only man in Heidelburg that has any money, and he is always willing to loan it to people. He more or less governs the town. Chris tells me I shouldn't talk about him, but we have been paying on the debt all these years, and he never has time to tell us how much we owe. Chris has always asked for a receipt, but Mr. Wilder (Boss Hogg, I call him) never likes to give him one. Anyway we've kept them all these years. He is even making us pay compound interest. He even looks like Boss Hogg, you remember him on "The Dukes of Hazard," don't you? You being a newspaper reporter, you probably don't have time to watch TV too much."

Matthew interrupted and told her he had watched the show many times, and at the same time he was connecting things in his mind. He asked Emily the man's name again and wrote it down. "I'm not the only one who calls him Boss Hogg," Emily said, "Everyone who owes him money has the same problem, draining everyone's pockets, barely leaving all of us enough to exist on."

Emily continued, "I got a job in a lunchroom in a country school and hoped he wouldn't find out I was working. We were needing our stove repaired; we only had one eye working. We were able to get the eyes replaced, and our refrigerator had gone out, and we were able to buy a good second-hand one. Our washing machine had conked out and we were able to get it fixed. I had been having to do our washing by hand. We were needing new tires on our truck, and we got new tires. Things were going smoothly for us, but Old Boss found out some way about me working. He came out here mad as an old setting hen, had his feathers all turned up, and asked about my job. After I told him it was true, I was working, he threatened to take our property from us for not turning the checks over to him.

"He buys eggs from us because he says he likes fresh ones. I heard he took them to town and sold them for twice what he pays us. After we heard about it, as far as he knows, the hens slacked off in laying, and he only got a small number of what the hens really laid. I quit my job at school, for I was tired of him getting everything we made. I can save money from the eggs and we were able to have a little extra for Christmas and bought each other a small gift. I look in the mail box around Christmas, Father's Day, Mother's Day, and on our birthdays. I don't want to be babyish but maybe I won't be forgotten. Anyway Chris and I have each other, and our sons have their families."

Matthew was getting very emotional. He wondered how three businessmen could become so engaged in their businesses that they would fail to send even a greeting card. "If they could see this house and hear the story Emily has just poured out to me." He thought, "I'll get their addresses one way or the other, for they must hear this story."

Emily said "I don't know why I'm pouring my heart out to you like I am. Maybe because you are a good listener. I'm afraid to trust anyone around here to tell them about our problems, for if Old Boss Hogg heard, he might come in and clean us out. When I was working I bought a home permanent and had a friend of mine put it in. One Saturday Chris and I went in to town, which we seldom get to do. Boss saw us across the street and yelled out at me and told me I had better be paying our debts than to have my hair all kinked up. It made Chris so mad, I was afraid he might cross the street and land a good one on him. I would have loved to see it happen had it not been for what he kept saying we owe him. He keeps taking most all of Chris' pay and allowing us only enough to barely get by. Our house is leaking and Chris asked if he could miss a few pay days so he could cover it. Boss said, "Oh it looks in good shape to me, you know I've got to live too. Just patch it up. It will last several years."

"He makes his unwanted visits out here often to see if we've made any changes. I don't know how he thinks we can. We have been having to wear clothes bought at yard sales since we borrowed money from Mr. Wilder. I see other women in pretty clothes, and their hair with permanents, and I cry. Maybe I'm just a big baby. I would like to be properly dressed one more time in my life."

Matthew knew then that this would be his story of the year. "Just wait until I get back to New York. I'll have one of the most heartwarming stories that has ever hit the press." He was so buried in his thoughts that he had forgotten to listen to Emily. After shaking off his trance, he asked Emily if they didn't care for TV. "Oh yes! We loved it, until it went out on us, and Mr. Wilder says we can live without TV and for us to try and get our debt paid off to him. Someday I hope we can look to the hills and mountains and be able to smile, knowing we are out of bondage to a person who only cares for himself, and I believe it will eventually come true. Chris doesn't say much about it, but at times I catch him in deep thoughts, and looking at him I can tell he would like to shake the demon right out of Mr. Wilder. Maybe someday someone will be able to do just that."

One day, for no particular reason he could think of, Paul Colby called his brothers Mark and Julian and said, "You know, we haven't been together since we graduated from college. Could we get together halfway between the three of us?" After making several telephone calls, they agreed on a location. Paul made the reservations and told them to be sure to bring their wives and children.

The time grew near and each one of them could hardly wait to get to see the others. Even the wives and children looked forward to going. Julian got there first with his wife Cathryn, their son Julian Jr., and daughter Katie. Mark came next with his wife Mary and daughter Maria, Paul finally made it with his wife Jane and their three children, Paul Jr. and twins Elizabeth and Emily. They were all busy, the men telling of their business experiences, and the in-laws getting acquainted, while the cousins were making so much noise the parents could hardly hear each other. Each of the brothers took turns telling of his business career, while the wives spoke of their social activities. The time seemed to fly by, and they had such a wonderful time together, they couldn't believe it was time to pack their suitcases and bid each other good-bye.

Before they left, Paul insisted they get together again soon. Going to Tennessee was on his mind, but he asked them to come to his house. He did say, "You know, the green hills of Tennessee haunt me sometimes." This brought back memories to Mark and Julian, and one of them asked, "When has anyone heard from Pop and Mom?" Each one looked to the other for an answer, and finally they spoke in unison: "I don't know, it's been years." Paul said, "I think it's time we start remembering."

After a pause, the men got in their cars where their wives and children were waiting. They all went home with light hearts and happy memories of the reunion.

It was getting around noon and Emily was wondering what she could cook Matthew for lunch. Most Southerners believe in feeding people. She asked to be excused while Matthew was busy writing notes. She hurriedly fried ham and made biscuits and gravy. She didn't want Matthew to see her run-down kitchen. She fixed a plate of the food and took it to him. The food was delicious, and he wished while he was eating that his wife could make biscuits like Emily could.

After eating he wondered if she had more to tell, and hinted this to her. She scratched her head and said, "I hate to tell you this, but we threatened to have our son Julian to check in on our business with Mr. Wilder, and of course Mr. Wilder didn't want that to happen. We had always kept our sons' addresses on the table, here in our living room. He had probably seen them before, as he is so nosy and had a great idea of swiping them. Well, he came out here one day and asked if we had any green beans for sale; he had no intention of paying for them, for he never did pay for the vegetables when he got them. Chris told him we had a few–we never let him know how much we have of things or he would take all we have. He said, "Chris old pal why don't you run out in the garden and help your wife pick me a good mess of fresh green beans. You know you should help her pick them." While we were gone the old rascal stole our sons' names with their addresses. He had no intention of letting Julian get hold of him. We don't have any way of getting in touch with our sons. All we know to do is to lift up out eyes to the hills from whence comes our help."

Matthew wanted to make sure he had the three sons' names and the locations correct and asked again for them. Emily remembered the town and state of each one, but said, "That is if they are still there. It has been so long since we've heard." Matthew knew the story had been beautifully told, and when he buttered it up, there would be thousands of papers sold. He had been greatly rewarded. He thanked Emily for the story she had bravely told, and also for the delicious meal she took time to prepare. As he left he gathered up the story he had jotted down, laid a twenty-dollar bill on the table, and started out. Emily saw the money and insisted on him taking it back, but being a persistent reporter, he won the argument. She finally accepted it, and said, "Well, I'll keep it and buy Chris a birthday present. His birthday is soon. I'll be so happy to have money to get him a gift." Matthew knew then that after forty years, Emily and Chris were still deeply in love.

Matthew left the home of Chris and Emily feeling sad for them and bitter toward Boss Hogg. It was a feeling he had never experienced. All the way back to New York he relived the stories Emily had told him. Even though their sons had seemed to forget them, she held nothing against them, and she felt sure that some time justice would come and she and Chris would be able to live with full paychecks, and Boss Hogg would get his share of embarrassment for the wrongs he had done to them and to others.

Matthew felt so rewarded as he pulled into his driveway in New York, and Carrie (his wife) and little Joy, his daughter, met him with smiling faces. Jo'y was not only smiling, but she had her mouth covered with peanut butter and jelly from the sandwich she was eating, Matthew was so glad to see them that he didn't mind a jelly kiss at all, and he kissed Carrie and got jelly and peanut butter on her mouth, too. Matthew very seldom told Carrie stories from his interviews, but this one was so different and intriguing he just had to tell her.

The next morning Matthew got to the office early, before the janitor got through cleaning. He was so anxious to get his story in print that he had left home without his billfold, which contained his drivers license. When he remembered it, he was glad he hadn't been stopped by a cop. He called Carrie and asked if she'd please bring it to him. She was more than pleased to get to bring it, hoping she could hear some more of the story he was preparing to print. No one else was around when she arrived, so he told her some more.

His story was of picturesque scenes of the rolling green hills and the scalloped blue mountains of east Tennessee. He described the shabby house that poor Emily and Chris were forced to live in and call home. Carrie was so enthralled by Matthew's descriptions Matthew had just given her, she felt as if she were there with Emily. She wished she could do something, and she asked Matthew just that. "Well," said Matthew, "I have a plan for my story. We'll just wait and see, so I must get to work." He kissed Carrie and opened the door for her and told her he must get to work on his long story.

Carrie drove back home feeling very depressed over the story Matthew had told her. All her life she had gotten most everything she had ever wanted, and thinking of people having to live in poverty over someone's greed for money was so hard. She said a little prayer asking God to help this couple get away from this greedy man. She felt much relieved after her short prayer. After getting home and having a cup of mocha, Carrie read Joy some stories.

Matthew worked all day and into the night, taking time off to eat and call Carrie; he told her to not be uneasy, for he had to keep working on the story he had brought back and would get home very late. He wanted the story to touch the hearts of everyone who read it. He couldn't have it ready for Wednesday, but Thursday it made headlines. After the editor read it, he knew a story like this would sell and he had a number of extra copies made. The headline read "Man of Power in Tennessee Drains Couple of Money." The article was long, and Matthew left nothing out.

Julian came home from a frustrating day's work. Everything had gone wrong. His clients weren't cooperative and his secretary went home sick at noon. After kicking off his shoes and picking up the daily paper, he flopped down in a recliner in the den. Cathryn saw the look in his eyes that she had seen many times before, and she backed off into the kitchen. She knew he would soften up after he had a glass of tea and a few minutes to relax. As she handed him the tea, she glanced over his shoulder, reading the headline in the paper. She saw the word "Tennessee" and looked more closely. Julian looked up at Cathryn and said, "I know of that reporter. He's supposed to be one of the best news reporters the Times has ever had." He asked Cathryn if she would like for him to read the article out loud. "Why yes," replied Cathryn, "I love having you read to me." Something within her told her it was something special.

As Julian read, every line brought him to knowing the couple in the story must be his parents. Then what popped up? The names of three sons, Julian, Mark, and Paul, with a brief description of each one and what businesses they were engaged in. Reading on he saw it wasn't just heartbreaking but embarrassing, not only for his wife to see how neglectful he had been, but for his friends and associates. How could he face the public knowing so many people would read it? After reading the last line, he put his arm around Cathryn and said, "What a bum son I have turned out to be, not only me, but my two brothers also. Mom and Dad sacrificed everything they had for us, not letting us know what John Wilder was doing to them. They told us they worked and lived for our happiness."

Cathryn interrupted and asked Julian just when he had last contacted his parents. With a deep look in his eyes he answered, "I don't know, but I will soon. I'm calling Mark and Paul right now." Cathryn interrupted again and said that they had to eat supper before it got cold. Cathryn had never seen Julian eat so fast, or see his face so red; his Scotch-Irish temper really popped out. After swallowing the last bite, he rushed to the telephone. He called Mark first and told him about the newspaper article. He added, "There is nothing I would rather do right now than to cram a box of cigars down the throat of Boss Hogg, as Mom calls him, and when I get there, I might do some cramming."

Mark tried calming his brother down, but it was impossible. Mark told Julian to talk with Paul and then they would make plans. When Paul's telephone rang, he knew by the tone of Julian's voice that something had happened. After hearing the story, Paul suggested the three of them take some time off and head for Indian Gap. They exchanged many telephone conversations until their schedules were all worked out, and then they packed their bags and headed home together.

Big plans were made. Julian took the job of straightening Mr. Wilder out; he was a lawyer, so Mark and Paul knew he could do it. The miles sped by and three tired brothers neared Indian Gap, the place they used to call home. As they turned in the driveway they saw the rusty old mail box without the flag, and "Emily and Chris Colby" printed on it in bold red letters. Paul said, "Dad and Mom and the beaten up mail box, how sad! Why have we . . . ?" and then stopped talking.

As they drove up the hill Mark asked Paul, "What has happened to the grape vine we used to swing on?" Paul said, "Yes, and remember throwing rocks in the creek to see the ripples? Julian, remember how we would slide down the bank and stop just in time to keep from going in the creek?" Soon they were in sight of the tumbledown house.

Emily was standing by the window, looking over the hills as she had done so many times, thinking that some day their sons would come back. The tree-lined bumpy road kept her from seeing Chris when he came home from work. They seldom had company, unless you could call Boss Hogg company. He came often, not to visit but to pry their personal business. Now Emily glimpsed a car which was not Chris's beat-up truck but a shiny new car. Emily heard the motor cut off and thought she should go to the door. She ventured out, and three young men got out of the car and walked up through the yard. As they got closer to the broken-down porch, Emily recognized them and screamed with delight. Chill bumps came over her and tears streamed down her face. She said, "I have always told the hills that some day our sons would come back." Emily wasn't the only one crying.

Emily warned the young men to be careful how they stepped on the porch or they might fall in. Not long afterward, Chris drove up. He was wondering who was there in a nice car like that. When they heard their dad's truck pull up the three men rushed out to meet him, and more tears were shed. After hugs and handshakes, Chris said, "So this is why I've had you boys on my mind all day." Julian told them of the newspaper article and how they planned to choke old Boss Hogg on his cigar if he didn't clear things up. Then Dad caught them up on local happenings while Mom prepared a good Southern supper such as the boys hadn't had for so many years.

While Julian went through all the receipts, Paul helped Mom with the dishes the way he used to do. Mark walked over the farm and returned in time to hear Dad tell how awful Mr. Wilder had treated them. He didn't know this was in the paper, and he told again of how they had worn clothes bought at yard sales these past years, and how Mom had wished for a new dress and shoes and how much she wanted a permanent. Paul thought of how he used to tell his mom when he was growing up that when he had loads of money he'd build them a new house. Mark was thinking too of the plans the brothers had made coming home.

With fingers trembling with anger, Julian ran all the receipts up and came up with a big surprise. He said, "If old man Wilder rejects my figures, I'll sue him and maybe send him to prison. My figures show you'll be getting back money." It was getting late and Chris had to go to work the next day. The three men had much to see to. They were tired and needed to go to bed. Mom turned their covers back just as she used to do, and the men crawled onto the worn-out mattresses they had slept on many years ago. Mom's three little boys fell asleep.

It was good to be back home again on the lumpy mattresses that had been home for them for so many years. Morning came much too soon and the noise from Chris's old truck woke them up as he left for work. After getting up and going out to the outside toilet, the three men ate the good breakfast Mom had prepared for them. Julian and Mark were soon headed for town. Paul stayed home for a purpose, as his plans were multiplying like rabbits.

Mom told Paul she hoped Julian could get things straightened out so they could buy some things they needed. Paul assured mom things would be smoothed out. Mom said, "We need so many things, a new roof on the house, new rugs, paint for the walls, electrical appliances . . . " Then she said, "I'd love to have a new TV and get the bathroom fixtures replaced. And then there's Chris's truck. It is falling apart." Paul just then noticed the rug with worn-out places in it. He said, "Mom, if I know my brothers like I think I know them, things will soon be going smoothly."

Paul had been outside looking over the yard, especially where the water line ran from the pump house. He checked the line to the septic tank and marked it off with sticks. Mom wondered what he was doing but kept quiet.

It was getting up in the afternoon and Julian and Mark hadn't gotten back from town. Emily and Paul were both getting a little anxious, not knowing what might have happened between Julian and Mr. Wilder. Paul called to Mom and said, "Quit your worrying. Here they come now." Mom met them at the door, very anxious to hear their story. Mark (as always) had to tease Mom and told her everything was settled, but they still owed Boss Hogg $5000. Poor Emily looked disappointed and said, "We'll never get out of debt." Julian said, "Mom, Mark is still his old self and he still has to tease you, but things aren't nearly so bad. Look at this check made out to Dad for $10,000." Mom was so thrilled. Her first thought was that Chris could buy a second-hand car and if there was any money left they could have the house covered. Emily always thought of Chris' needs first.

Julian told Mom to sit down on the couch with the springs coming through the upholstery. She did, and Julian told the story. "As Mark and I walked into Mr. Wilder's office," Julian began, "He was busy arguing with a man, telling him he would have to take him to court if the man didn't have the money for the interest on the money he owed Mr. Wilder by tomorrow. Boss looked up at us and finally recognized us. By the look on his face he knew his goose was cooked. He jumped up from his chair, shook our hands, hugged us, and started pouring compliments on us thicker than molasses on a cold morning. He started bragging about you and Dad being such good, honest, hard-working people. He was getting jittery, and he stuttered.

"We let him bestow all the flimsy compliments on us he could think of. Stopping for a second to chew on his cigar, he gave Julian a chance to take over and start talking business. Mr. Wilder tried to say the receipts Chris had kept were fakes, even if he had signed them himself. Julian interrupted and asked Mr. Wilder if he had forgotten that Julian was a lawyer. He also assured Mr. Wilder that he had made no mistakes in figures. "You very well know I could take you to court and sue you for all the unlawful things you've done to take advantage of my parents," Julian said. Then Julian told Mark to call the gentleman who had been in the office back in before he got away. Julian said, "Mr. Wilder, before he comes back in, just go ahead and write a check made out to my father, Chris

Colby, for $10,000, and consider yourself getting off easy." Mr. Wilder was getting pale and jittery, chewing on his cigar, and saying, 'You are going to ruin me.' Julian said, "Yes, as you have ruined my father. Now write the check, or go to court."

Boss wrote the check and by the handwriting anyone could tell he was quite shaken up. Julian thanked him for he check, and asked for a receipt stating that his father's debt had been paid in full and had two witnesses verify it. Julian said, "We're not through yet. How about this gentleman you just threatened? Let's straighten things out with him. Would you mind letting me check his account?" Mr. Wilder was afraid to not let Julian check it, for he knew very well what Julian could do. Julian asked the man how much he owed Mr. Wilder, and he said, "The way I counted, I paid him off a long time ago." Julian checked the records and said, "Oh yes, you have paid your debt off some time ago." Julian turned to Mr. Wilder and said, "Write another check, Mr. Wilder. He has overpaid you by $2000." Seeing the scornful look in Julian's eyes, and knowing it was best to not disagree with a lawyer, he wrote the check while Julian looked over his shoulder to see if he had written it correctly. Julian said, "Don't forget to write the receipt and be sure to say paid in full," which Mr. Wilder did. The gentleman thanked Julian, and left with a very pleased look on his face.

Julian told Mr. Wilder, "I want to see you in church, and I want you to make a confession in front of all the members and promise to make it up to all the people you have cheated through the years." Mr. Wilder stammered, and said, "I could never do that. What would the preacher say? Besides that, I'd be ruined financially forever." Julian said, "You've had no mercy on my parents, so suit yourself in doing what I have asked you to do, or I'll take further action. I'll be at church Sunday, and I hope to see you there." Mr. Wilder had never had anyone to put it to him in such a daring way like that before. He was scared and he knew his cheating was over. He promised he'd be there."

Julian, Mark, and Paul were sitting on the front porch, which was falling down, while Mom was busy in the kitchen preparing a good country dinner. The men made plans about what to do first. Soon they heard the pickup truck coming up the drive way. Chris was thrilled to see his three sons sitting on their porch again. He sure didn't know their plans, and neither did mom. Emily finally had the meal prepared and called the four hungry men in to eat. While they were eating Julian told Chris all about his experience with Mr. Wilder and how he had saved another man from being drained of money, and then he handed Chris a check. Chris could hardly believe his eyes when he saw a $10,000 check made out to him. "Is it settled?" Chris asked. "Yes," said Julian, "From now on your paychecks will be yours. I took care of all that, and here is a receipt. All is clear between you and Mr. Wilder now."

Mark and Paul both spoke at the same time, "We have a little surprise for you both. We've been talking it over and we see how the house is almost beyond repair. How would you like for the three of us to buy you a new double-wide trailer?" Julian told them he and Mark had checked with a man Mark had graduated from high school with, and they had planned everything out. "Paul stayed here while we went into town to decide on where to put it. Is that is O.K. with you both?"

Chris and Emily both spoke at the same time, "We can't have you doing that. We can fix this place up now that we are out of debt." The boys all spoke and said, "It's too late now. The men are coming tomorrow to check if Paul has chosen the right place for it."

Paul said, "Mom, do you remember when I was growing up, I told you when I became a man and had loads of money, I'd build you and dad a new house? Well, it is not exactly that way, since I don't have loads of money, but the three of us have bought the double-wide."

Chris got up early the next morning and went in to work, and for the first time in years, he asked off for a few days to be with his sons, for he had no worry of old Boss ever again.

Friday came, and it was a busy day. Paul insisted on taking Chris and Emily to a town bigger than Heidelburg. They didn't know why he was taking them when the new house was being brought in, but they went along. Paul took them to a nice mall in the town. He found a nice store, and he asked a clerk to fit his mother in a new dress. She chose a navy dress and navy shoes and a navy bag. Dad chose a navy suit, new shirt, tie, and black shoes. While they were there Paul took them to a restaurant for lunch.

Emily said, "Paul, you have made us so happy, I feel like I'm dreaming." Chris laughed and said, "Can I pinch you so you can tell if you're dreaming or not?" Emily said, "No, Paul, it's real. I know it's real." On the way home they told Paul that these were the first new outfits they'd bought since Julian finished high school. When they came through Heidelburg Paul stopped at a beauty shop and went in. When he came out he gave Emily a certificate to get a permanent the next day at 9:30 a.m. He asked Chris if he could bring her in and said, "You need a haircut yourself; here's the money for that." Then he told them he would be helping them with things around the house. Chris and Emily were so happy that nothing seemed real.

As they drove up the driveway they saw that the house had been delivered and assembled. Everyone had worked real hard: the electricity had been turned on and the plumbers had connected the water. The boys told their dad that he could add a porch, but for now they would have to do with the steps the workers had brought. Chris and Emily stood staring with unbelieving eyes. The boys said, "Go on in and look it over." There it was: floors covered in carpets and tile, two baths, new stove, refrigerator, dining set, couch, chairs, tables, lamps, one new bedroom suite with a queen-size bed and a good mattress. Like all trailers, it was furnished with shades and drapes. But they didn't sleep in the double-wide that night. They all wanted to sleep in the old house as long as the boys stayed, for they knew it would be torn down soon.

Saturday morning came and Emily was anxious to go into town for her permanent. She could hardly wait. Chris took her to the beauty shop and then went for a haircut. He picked Emily up later, and while they were driving home Chris complimented Emily on her new hairstyle and told her how pretty she looked. Emily looked at Chris and said, "Chris, you know you are as handsome as you were forty years ago."

As they came to their house, they didn't see anyone around. It looked almost deserted, but while they were gone Julian and Mark had rushed into town and bought a new TV and when they got to the door, they saw all three boys sprawled out on the chairs and couch watching boxing on TV. Just another big surprise! The boys told Dad and Mom how great they looked, with Dad's great haircut and Mom's new permanent.

When the boxing was over, the men moved the better pieces of furniture to the new house and saw the need for new mattresses for the two other beds. In fact they knew it after sleeping on them the first night. Mark took off in a rush to the furniture store, hoping the store would deliver the mattresses that day and, with a little persuasion, they did. After they were delivered, Mark told Julian and Paul he would get to sleep in the bed all to himself, and that's the way it was. Julian and Paul shared a bed and they decided to stay in the new house. It was nice getting to sleep in the new house and having inside bathrooms.

Time to get up and get ready for church. Sunday had come so quickly. Julian had been ready for it since he saw Mr. Wilder earlier in the week. When Mom and Dad came out dressed in their new outfits, the boys really gave them a boost by telling them enthusiactically how attractive they both looked.

The men had only casual clothes to wear, but even in these, they all looked sharp and handsome. They enjoyed seeing their old friends, and it was so nice to go to church once more with their parents. Julian started twisting before the preacher quit preaching. He was so afraid Mr. Wilder wouldn't have a chance to confess or that he might sneak out before the Preacher closed. Finally the Preacher asked if anyone had any confessions to make. Julian glanced around to make sure Boss would come forward. Mr. Wilder stood up and made his flimsy speech. He said he had always tried to be good and helpful to people, and that he had helped financially, but had made a terrible mistake in figures with a dear friend. But he had corrected it, and hoped he was forgiven. He sat down.

The man Julian had helped get his money back from Boss stood up and said that Mr. Wilder made the same mistake with him, and he wanted to thank Julian Colby for getting some of his money back. Another man arose and said he wished he'd gone over his bills again. He had barely sat down when a big muscular woman with a ruddy complexion, deep blue eyes, and stringy blonde hair arose from her seat and faced the audience. Shaking her finger in Boss' direction, she said, "You old codger, you have beat everybody in this here town out of money. Tomorrow me and Claude is coming to your office and you better be ready to clear things up with us." The preacher was afraid a free-for-all was about to begin, and he said, "If no one else has anything to say, we'll sing the closing song and consider ourselves dismissed."

The boys enjoyed talking with everyone, and everyone complimented Chris and Emily on their good looks. People whispered to each other about why Boss confessed, although the smarter ones had it figured out.

After eating lunch at Shoney's the Colbys went home feeling full and happy. Mr. Wilder, on the other hand, went home with a guilty feeling, scared that all whom he had cheated might play the same game Julian played. Maybe some of them weren't so smart. A verse in the Bible popped into Mr. Wilder's mind: "Whatsoever you sow, that shall you also reap." Soon he, too, might be living in a leaky house, just as he had caused others to have to do.

The boys were well pleased with everything they had carried out, but they were a little anxious to see their families, so they decided to leave the next morning. The time had been so short, but look what they had accomplished! A dream house and happy parents. Yes, they must go home. Kissing each other good bye, they started to the car.

Paul turned around and with a quivery voice said, "Dad, now that you have money and a good pay day, please have a telephone put in, so we can all keep in touch." Paul gave each of their telephone numbers to Emily, and kissed her again. Then the three sons drove away. Chris and Emily watched as they drove out of sight. Chris gave Emily a big hug and also a great big highschool kiss and said, "I feel as young as I did when we were dating in highschool." Emily looked up at him with a big smile, and Chris knew she felt the same way. The heavy load had finally been lifted, and they could always thank Julian for the good lesson he had taught Boss Hogg. They were hoping Boss wouldn't forget and cheat someone else out of their life's savings. Chris said, "Let's just forget Boss and all that's happened, for after all he did loan us the money."

Emily made a fresh pot of coffee and called Chris into the kitchen. She set out a plate of cookies, and she and Chris sat at the kitchen table, drinking coffee and eating cookies, feeling very relaxed and happy. They were as happy as they had been more than 40 years ago, with much, much more experience. On the way home the three sons made plans to bring their wives and children to visit their parents, and to let them enjoy their grandchildren, as all grandparents want to do. And they all did just that, as the years passed by.

So long!

See ya!

YESTERDAY

October 15

Dear Fern,

Since I've kind of got caught up with my work, before winter jobs of quilting, crocheting, tatting, and the hard job of cracking walnuts, and helping get corn shucked, I'll try and write you a letter. I sure enjoyed hearing from you and all the news you told me.

It's been real rewarding for me this past year. In March I crossed the stage in Wyanona High School and got my diploma; eleven other girls and boys received theirs, too. That was the biggest class that has graduated from Wyanona. What really hurt me most in graduating was leaving Emory. We became very close friends. Confidentially, it's a little more than friendship. Maybe some day you will have the opportunity of meeting him. He's tall (six feet and four inches), has blue eyes and sandy hair and is very handsome. He plans to go up north to get work. I hope I can talk him out of going. He lives in Pine Cove, about five miles from here.

As we parted from school, he put his arm on my shoulders and brushed a lock of my hair back in place. He left the impression he'd be seeing me soon. I watched the mail daily, hoping I would hear from him. Finally a letter came with the post mark 'Pine Cove.' I tore the envelope open very quickly. My heart was pounding and I could hardly wait to read the contents. I won't go into details as to what he wrote, but I will say it was sweet as honey. He asked me to answer real soon, and believe me I did. Here is something he said that I just have to tell you. He said, "Frances, my dear, I can hardly wait to see you again, I want to take you in my arms and hold you close to me." He also told me he had his sorrel horse shod, and he's ready to go, and please answer soon. Believe me, I had a two cent stamp on an envelope addressed to him the next day.

Saturday I cleaned the parlor up real good, took the rug up and put it on the clothes line and beat the dust out, dusted the sofa, organ and center table, then I put the rug down. I also cleaned the lamp globes real good and filled them up with kerosene. I put the picture I had made of myself on the organ. I had a feeling if he saw it he might want it.

Mama thought I should have some refreshments to serve him. Papa was going in to town for some things he needed on the farm, and I asked him to get lemons, so I could make lemonade. I made an egg custard and it turned out to be very delicious.

I took a bath in the wash tub and washed my hair, and after it dried I started dressing. You remember the pretty pink blouse I have–you know, it has all the pretty lace and tucks on it–then I put my blue serge skirt on. I wore my corset, as I wanted to look slim and pretty. Next I put on my gray spool heel shoes. Mama had me wear her Cameo pin; she said that was for good luck since Papa gave it to her when they first started sparking. Next I combed my hair, and then tatted it, making big puffs over my ears (you know how stylish it is now) and the rest of my hair I put in a neat ball on the back of my neck. To finish up, I put starch on my face and looked real pale and delicate.

Oh, I must tell you I went to a dentist a few months back, and he put a gold crown on one of my front teeth, and that helped to set me off. It sure seems like I'm bragging about myself. I'm just so happy I have to tell someone and you being my best friend–hope you don't mind.

Anyway, I was getting so anxious to see Emory, and all at once I saw a sorrel horse turn the curve of the road. I knew it had to be him. I kept peeping through our crocheted window curtains watching him come up the road. Finally he reached the hitching post and got off his horse and started to the house. Was he ever dressed up! He had a navy blue serge suit on, black laced shoes, a blue striped shirt with an extra stiff starched collar, and a dark blue bow tie. He even had a derby hat. Oh how I wanted to run out and fall in his arms, but I knew papa and mama would object–they'd think I was being fast. I only let him knock once, and believe me, the door flew open. As soon as the door was closed Emory grabbed me in his arms, kissing me so affectionately and telling me he loved me and had missed seeing me. It was like heaven, being in his arms, and hearing words so beautifully spoken.

He bragged about the egg custard and lemonade being so good. He said, "I see right now you're a good cook." You know, that sounded kind of promising to me.

Time passed so quickly, and I heard the clock strike ten. I heard Papa clear his throat and cough a time or two, and I knew that was a signal to tell Emory it was time to go. I followed him up to the door and stood in his arms until I was afraid Papa would cough again. But after all, I am 21! I was glad that the moon was shining bright so Emory wouldn't have to carry a lantern to see to get home. I watched him as far as I could see him, and then listened to his horse's hoofs as they went trotting down the road. I came back in the house feeling happier than I had ever been in my life. For this was the first time I had really been in love, and I knew Emory loved me.

I got the lamp and went upstairs to my cold bedroom. I removed my clothes and got into a warm gown, combed out my hair, and crawled into my straw mattress. I said my prayers and thanked God for giving me Emory, even if it was just for the night. But you know how greedy people are: I had to ask for more. I said, "Please don't let this be the last time for me to be with him." Deep in my heart I wanted to ask God to give him to me now.

The moon was still shining, spreading beams of light through the window and making shadows of a tree outside my window. Sleep just wouldn't come. I tossed and turned and relived every moment we had spent together, especially the warm kisses he had put on my lips. Finally, in the wee hours of morning, I fell into a peaceful sleep.

It seemed such a short time until papa was calling for us girls to get up and help mama get breakfast or we would be late for church. Oh, how I wished for

Emily and Susan to tell me I could sleep in, but sometimes sisters are not too cooperative, and I had to hit the cold floor too. Everything went off fine, and Papa didn't complain about Emory staying a little after ten. My brothers Joe and Maurice kind of kidded me about Emory; they didn't know how much I enjoyed it.

Mama had cooked pork ribs, green beans, and baked sweet potatoes on Saturday to have for lunch on Sunday. She always makes light bread to have to eat over the weekend when the temperature is warm enough for the bread to rise.

We all hurried around and dressed for church. We had to be on time, since Papa leads the singing and Emily plays the organ. Joe and Maurice harnessed up the horses for the surrey for Papa, Mama and us girls to ride in, then they saddled up their horses and we all started off to church together. Emily, Susan, Mama and me all wore our feather-trimmed hats, and mama wore the fox stole that Aunt Laura left for her when she died. It was cool enough that mama thought she wouldn't be improperly dressed.

We made it on time and Papa and Emily started the music. Papa was standing up front keeping time to the music and singing as Emily bore down on the peddles on the organ. The first song was "In the Sweet Bye and Bye," which seems to be everybody's favorite. Emily was doing her best at playing and Papa was really bellowing out singing. It seemed like everybody was so happy. Maybe it was because I was so happy. Sometimes your attitude can cause other people to seem different. Uncle Jesse didn't even nod, and John Stiles was so involved in the singing and preaching that a wasp built its nest in what little bit of hair he has left and he didn't even feel it. (Fern that really didn't happen about the wasp. I'm just so happy over Emory I'm likely to write anything.)

November 24

Fern I'm so ashamed I haven't gotten this letter in the mail, but time gets away. I am so busy now. Mama helped me put the quilting frames up, and I put my "Lone Star" quilt I had pieced some time ago in the frames, and Mama,

Emily, Susan and I have been quilting on it. I thought of having a quilting party but some women think they can quilt when they can't. I wanted all the stitches small and dainty.

Fern, it is one of my prize quilts. I have it hemmed and put in my trunk. I thought while I was putting it away just how pretty it would look spread over Emory, if he was taking a nap. Maybe someday I will get to experience it. Speaking of Emory, he has been back six times since I started this letter. I'll tell you, he gets sweeter every time I see him. To me he's the only thing sweeter than honey. He keeps saying he's going to Detroit, Michigan to get a job in Henry Ford's factory making cars. He has big dreams, and he said if he did go and get a job, he'd buy a car, pay for it, and then work for money to build us a house. He said he didn't want me to have to ride a horse or ride in a buggy or surrey. It sounds awfully good, but I know my heart would just break to see him get on a train and head for Detroit. But the newspapers say there's plenty of work there, and they pay good.

Guess I had better stop and help Emily and Susan scour the kitchen, so they'll help me put my double wedding ring quilt in the frame. They have been real good in helping me quilt. I also have four sets of pillow cases and matching bolster cases. I have tatting on two sets and crocheting on the other two. I also have dresser scarves to match the pillow cases. As you can read, I haven't been wasting my time. I also have a chicken feather bed and two goose feather pillows. Grandma Nease gave me two flax sheets that she had made many years ago. I really treasure them, for making flax cloth is something that has gone out. Mama still raises cotton and uses it for batting to pad quilts with.

I'm considering teaching school next fall if I can get a school close to home. That is if Emory goes to Detroit. I think the county pays twenty dollars a month. They may pay more for high school graduates. I'll have to ride a horse and that would mean I'd have to buy a side saddle. It would never do to go to school and let my students se me ride astride.

Still Later

Christmas and Thanksgiving have passed and Emory did go to Detroit. He really likes his job but misses me as much as I miss him (I hope). He writes often, and so do I.

Oh, I must tell you what he gave me for Christmas: a beautiful 14K gold locket with his picture in it and a matching brooch! And that's not all— he gave me a pretty matching scarf and gloves. They are wool and in mingled shades of blue.

In his last letter he asked me for my ring size (for my ring finger) and even asked if I'd rather have a ruby or diamond. I answered and sent my ring size, and I told him that I like rubies but my heart goes out for diamonds. He plans to come back in late March, and here I go hoping he'll propose. He kind of hinted he might be driving a new T model Ford. I think they cost around four hundred dollars. That's big money but he's making good; he's been working six days a week. I feel uneasy for him. He'll have to learn to drive and patch inner tubes and change tires. Maybe by late March the weather will be getting pretty and he won't have to drive over ice. He says the weather up there is really rough, colder and with more snow than we have here in Tennessee. Speaking of the weather here, we sure have had a rough winter so far. Seems like all the men can get done is cut wood. I was proud we got the tobacco worked off before it got so cold. The creeks have frozen over and the men folk have to cut holes in the ice for the cattle to drink. They have been doing that for the past two weeks. All we women can do is sit by the fire and try to stay warm.

Influenza is raging everywhere, but we're trying to escape it. Every time any of us seems to be taking a cold, Mama goes for the century plant and makes tea for us to drink. It's as bitter as quinine, but it sure breaks up a cold.

Later Again

Here it is March and I hope winter is over. It sure was a snowy, rough winter, but signs of spring seem to be everywhere: the tulips, crocus, and daffodils are all in full bloom, while the bees are busy buzzing around stealing the nectar from the flowers.

I'm trying to get ready for Easter, March 26. Emory is coming home and will be driving his new T model Ford. I'll be uneasy until he gets here, for he hasn't been driving long. After learning to drive in Detroit I guess he ought to make it to Tennessee. He said the roads were paved there. I didn't hardly know what he meant by a paved road.

I have my Easter outfit all ready, I ordered my dress from Montgomery and Ward; it is a pale blue linen, it has a white eyelet collar and cuffs, and has a wide white leather belt. It has a real tight skirt that comes almost to my ankles. My hat is the same shade of blue. I found it in a store in town, and it has a wide brim with pink and white roses around the crown and a white veil which covers my chin. My slippers are white with two straps across them and buttons on the side. I bought a pair of white silk stockings and had to give thirty nine cents for them.

I sure hope Emory likes my outfit. I can hardly wait for him to get here, and it will be nice to see his new car and go to church with him. I hope I can go alone with him. Just think of getting to ride up to the church and having everybody seeing him open the door and help me out! Everybody else will be in buggies, surreys, or hacks or riding horses. Here's something else to think about: what if the sound of the car scares the horses? There could be a stampede! Anyway, I'll wait and see and expect the best.

Few Weeks after Easter

Everything turned out just wonderful. Emory came and didn't have any problems at all. He didn't even get kicked cranking his car, which was great. You know Fern, he is more handsome than ever. When he got dressed for church he looked like a million dollar lawyer. We went to church and it being Easter Sunday all the ladies had their new Easter outfits on. Emory thought I was the prettiest and best dressed lady there.

Emory stopped the car just in time to keep Uncle Fred's horse from getting scared and running away in front of all the men who were standing outside getting their last chew of tobacco and smoking their roll-your-own stud cigarettes before going in to church. Some of the young girls were still outside hanging around the young boys, and they were all looking at us. Just as I hoped for, Emory got out came around and opened the door and helped me out. I felt like I was walking on higher ground.

Since it was Easter Sunday everybody had turned out, and the seats were all full in the back and near the front too. As we walked up the aisle I could tell everyone was gazing at us. I didn't know if they were looking at Emory or at me in my new outfit. We found a seat up front and sat down. After Emily played Easter songs, the preacher started preaching, and he preached and preached. It got kind of hot in the church and a deacon passed out Garret Snuff fans to the parishioners. Emory fanned me and I thought that was sweet. To tell the truth, I was so carried away I'm not sure if the preacher preached about Easter or Christmas.

I've kept you waiting for the good part long enough. Emory took my hand in his before we started to church, took a little box out of his pocket, and, guess what was in it–if you guessed a diamond then you're right. He put it on my finger and it fit perfectly. I was so happy that I cried. Then he asked me a question, "Will you marry me?" There's no way I would ever say no. I said, "Emory, darling, I'd marry you today if we had the marriage license." He laughed heartily and told me he had gotten it yesterday. He said, "I have a wedding band, too."

When the preacher asked if anyone had anything to say, Emory rose from his seat and said, "Reverend Farnsworth I have something to ask you." The Reverend told him to go ahead. Emory asked if he would marry us immediately after the service ended. Mama and Papa looked stunned; they didn't expect a marriage so soon.

Anyway we were married, and I didn't get married in white. But blue stands for always be true. So what more could we ask for? Everybody was shaking our hands and wishing us the best of luck after the wedding. It was late when we got back home, and Mama, Susan, and Emily finished up lunch in a hurry. It was delicious but I was just too much in love to eat. Mama apologized and said she wouldn't have time to prepare an entire supper, but we didn't mind at all.

The next morning we packed all we could put in the car and headed out for Detroit. It was a great experience for me, as I had never been further than Frankfort, Kentucky in my life. The trip was tiresome and it took a long time to get there. Emory had rented a three room apartment that has a bath and electric lights. The lights are so bright they hurt my eyes for a while, but I am getting adjusted to the brightness now.

It is just wonderful being here with Emory and I just hope we'll never be separated from each other again. It's time I started supper. Emory will be home soon, and I want to have supper prepared when he gets home.

Write me when you can, and hope you find someone that is as sweet as my Emory.

Sincerely, Francis and Emory Mabry

So long!

See ya!

FALLING OF THE LEAVES

Winter was almost over, and the cold days were turning into warm and sunny days of beauty. Many living things were resurrected. The dark clouds of winter had vanished.

The blue sky was a great wide field of promise and hope, where only a few floating white clouds mingled.

The huge poplar tree that had nestled the birds for many years, cradled the baby squirrels, and heard the humming of the bees, the songs of the chickadees, and the cooing of the lonely doves was a tranquil place for all living things to enjoy. The big winged eagle also makes its nest in the taller branches. The tree knew it was time again to reach out and collect food for the buds that were beginning to form. The warm spring weather was swelling the buds on the plants and trees everywhere.

The old branches from this particular tree had fallen away and new ones had replaced them. Days passed and the buds were bursting open; the leaves were beginning to show. Each individual leaf made its own pattern. Some were crumpled, and some had uneven edges, and others were perfect examples of their particular form.

As the late spring days grew longer, the hot sunshine helped the leaves grow to maturity. They shimmered and quivered in the gentle breeze, offering their shade to the weary passersby as they stopped for a cool and peaceful place to rest. As the rains came, the umbrella of leaves provided a shelter for whomever happened to be near.

Children loved the big, strong tree with its beautiful leaves, so slick and shiny, and enjoyed playing games under its shade. Many other memorable moments had also been experienced under the great tree. Some had been painful, as when two sweethearts had broken away from each other and said their last goodbyes. And many hearts had been warmed as couples sat together under the shade listening to the music of outdoor life. The tree stood firm and strong, never revealing any secrets that had been spoken. On its bark the tree bore the initials of many sweethearts.

Summer was almost over, and the leaves were taking on a different hue. What once was a shiny green was now a fallish yellow. Some leaves had already been taken away by the early fall winds. The harsh winds began to blow, the life the leaves lived was almost over. The leaves were a wrinkled, disheveled brown. It was time for the remaining leaf family to bid each one adieu.

Slowly they fell to the ground, covering each other in their own graves. A few, who had been good in their leafy way, were caught in a peaceful wind and carried to the river, where they were safely taken ashore to the other side. There the "Great Tree of Life" gathered them up and placed them securely in its branches, where they will remain forever.

Then we ask, "What is life?" It is the falling of the leaves. The beginning of a new life. Our lives.

So long!

See ya!

FATHER TIME

How do you describe "Father Time"? Is he a well-dressed man, well-groomed, rushing along with a briefcase, looking at no one, and wearing a look of uncertainty? Or maybe wearing a smile and seeming to know exactly where he's going? Or could he be the man in faded jeans, sweatshirt, and Nike shoes? No, that doesn't seem like Father Time. Maybe he's the stooped old man with a long white beard walking with a cane.

Really, I think you are all wrong. I ask a question: has anyone ever seen Father Time? The answer is no, but he has been here since God started making the world. Who has an exact answer to that? We know that time is the way we measure human life. Yet time is also the duration of all things; time has been through eternity and will continue to go on. To some it is so brief; for instance a baby's life can be snatched away and we are not big enough to understand why. Yet others are spared years, many years while time takes its toll, and you wonder if it would have been better to have never been born than to pay the price for something time permitted to be placed upon a human being.

Time is no respector of persons. While we're young, time seems to be on wings, waiting for no one. We rush to keep up, grabbing for the immeasurable amounts of fame and fortune to gratify our desires. Yet Father Time keeps going while you become old and bent. Then time seems to become slow. Everything is different; friends and loved ones have gone on with time, and you are left just waiting for the time that you, too, can go on to reap your reward. We know that time cannot be seen. We only endure it.

Now let's consider the wind. We need fresh air. We feel it. We need it to breathe. So we might ask, who has seen the wind? Neither I nor you, but when the trees bow down their heads the wind is passing through. What would happen to time if we had no air?

Here we have time and air, which we can't see but we know they are with us. And think about the spirit within us. Doctors never replace a spirit. That's something they have never found. It is invisible, but it is the most important of the three things that make up our great world: time, air, and our spirit which God only knows. God is the greatest of all beings. We can't see God, yet we know he is with us. Only infidels say there is no God.

God can be seen in so many different ways: in the voices of small children, or a baby's smile, or a good deed for a person. No, we don't see God as a person, but we know he's here with us. Without him there would be no time or air, but with his love and glory we know he's everywhere.

It is God who will take from our time-limited bodies, and will judge us for what we have done. If it's pure, our spirit will live on with the unmeasurable time that God has given us. And only the Great Physician can control the spirit.

So long!

See ya!